Wild Mushrooms

Wild Mushrooms

A Novel

E. PIOTROWICZ

RESOURCE *Publications* · Eugene, Oregon

WILD MUSHROOMS
A Novel

Resource Publications
An Imprint of Wipf and Stock Publishers
199 W. 8th Ave., Suite 3
Eugene, OR 97401

www.wipfandstock.com

PAPERBACK ISBN: 978-1-7252-6211-9
HARDCOVER ISBN: 978-1-7252-6212-6
EBOOK ISBN: 978-1-7252-6213-3

Manufactured in the U.S.A.   03/23/20

For Jesse with love

Contents

PART III—1976

PART 1—1974

1

The Beginning, The End, and Everything In-Between

IT WAS SURREAL, STRIKING, and bizarre: the perfect form, the smooth softness, the unexpected juxtaposition. A terrible wonder and illogical fear gripped me, as though my mortal flesh had been brushed by the immortal wing of a heavenly being. Would I be struck dead, consumed in flame for the impudence of touching eternity with soiled, temporal hands? It still projects itself upon my mind's eye some nights, that persistent memory so appallingly vivid—the vision of that ivory figure gleaming in the midsummer late-evening sun—naked like the blades of grass and the sun itself. But I'm losing myself in the artificial construct of chronology. What does it matter if I start at the beginning or the end or even the middle? It's all the same.

I was still a foreigner then. The long northwestern daylight hours had reached their apex, and the dark, drizzly winter remained nothing but a fragment of a recollection—a memory that melted into the mossy earth with the last grimy, crusts of old snow. There was only the sweet and glorious Now—the luminous lupine, hillocks plush with grass, and the sun, that yellow firebird finally come home after flying south for the winter.

I had come by Greyhound from New York, then boarded the ferry by foot, my heavy backpack digging trenches in my shoulders. The caffeine coursing through my veins masked the effects of sleep deprivation while suspending my brain in a haze of unreality. The landscape of towering evergreens, the sparkle of the sun on the strait of Juan de Fuca, all seemed to suggest some ethereal world, wholly other, but more real than myself. Voices entered and exited my consciousness without leaving behind any precise meaning—only sounds, intonations—a constant hum. The voices blended into the atmosphere like the ringing of cicadas or the chatter of early morning birdsong.

For years Erik had been inviting me to come and spend Midsummer at his cottage, situated on the largest of the San Juan Islands, nestled amid a densely forested piece of acreage on a lake. I was curious, which might have prompted me to accept his invitation sooner, had it not been for my persistent state of poverty since graduating from college. I was curious about his island at the country's extreme occident, but more curious still about Freja, whose beauty Erik had been describing in eloquence since their acquaintance.

My dream of visiting Erik in Washington had remained simply that, an unattainable fantasy. I was living in a grimy little loft in Greenwich, where I called myself an artist and paid the bills by helping fill prescriptions for my elderly neighbors and selling candy bars at the pharmacy across the street. I had begun several paintings that were meant to be masterpieces in their time but lost interest before I could finish them. Shards of my ambition littered the floor of my loft—roughly sketched on stretched canvas, then cast aside in despair. I waited—for inspiration, for the right subject, the right mental image, the right truth—but these, like the right woman, never came.

Loneliness gave way to sadness; sadness deepened into the dull and constant ache of depression, which unchecked, began to putrefy into something dangerously like despair. The weather didn't help my situation. I remember a dark, clammy, and unbearably lonely Saturday in February, my day off, with the icy blade of winter slowly cutting its way to my soul, when I started to consider. I sat sucking a cigarette, abstractedly pulling bits of white fluff from my old armchair, which sat by the only window facing the dingy side of the building next to mine. My mind seemed empty, shapeless, and colorless. I searched it for traces of originality, but every thought vanished before it could take shape, like drops of rain that fall in the desert, evaporating on contact. I considered throwing myself from the window and bashing my brains out on the pavement below, but I worried that I might somehow survive, fearing above all a vegetative existence devoid of movement or meaning, despite its likeness to my current condition. There are ways to be more confident of success in the business of self-slaughter, but I must not have been quite sad enough to consider them yet. I simply sat suspended in space.

I had a little money, (the cumulation of my Christmas bonus and the little bit I'd been able to save in an old coffee tin), and very little to lose. I made the decision right then at that moment—at 2:56 pm—there in my shabby chartreuse armchair, sucking on that cigarette, staring into space and semi-seriously contemplating suicide. I couldn't have predicted the events that decision would set into motion. No one could have. I decided, tremulously at first but with mounting confidence, to leave for a while— to spend the summer with Erik in Washington. Maybe getting away for a while would clear this mental obstruction. Maybe an escape was all I needed—some time with an old friend to rediscover forgotten truths and encounter new ones—to become inspired again. So I made a long-distance call to Erik, who responded with happy approval to my proposition. I arranged to arrive in early June, and the time leading up to my departure seemed somehow a little more bearable. It is monotony that crushes the soul, knowing that there is no end, no sunset, nothing to look forward to at the end of a long struggle. This trip was the sunset that promised both an end and, hopefully, a new beginning.

When the time came, as if I were analyzing an abstract art film, I watched myself board a greyhound bus, then board a ferry. I watched myself watch America fly by my window until finally reaching the thick, towering evergreen forests, and then the water. I watched myself breath in the smell of sunshine and saltwater from the upper deck of the ferry, the wind whipping through my hair and up my nostrils, with half-closed eyes. The screenplay was my own creation in which I had cast myself in the leading role. Now I looked through the lens as director, claiming control of the life I was acting out, and finally saw myself feel the movement of air—the movement of life. But I'd taken a long trip like this before—or was it someone else? Actually quite a bit longer. A weak memory that only flickers before my eyes dimly, usually only when I smell black tea and kabanos sausages. A train.

> Speeding past green trees reaching out of red earth into blue sky, the colors blended together. The little boy lay folded tightly in his mother's arms. They tried to sleep in their shared bunk as the train pitched, swayed, and periodically stopped in small towns along the way. Sleep wouldn't come. The little boy needed to use the lavatory but feared leaving the safety of their car. Babushka had told him to keep the door locked at all times. He squirmed uncomfortably.

"After today, things will be different. After today you won't be Eliasz anymore; no, not Ilyusha either. You'll be Elias. It means the same, my love, but it will be easier for them to say. We'll both work hard. We'll learn English, and we'll talk in that language together you and I. We'll get so good at it that no one will know you weren't born speaking it. You'll go to school . . . maybe college and have so many opportunities—things you could never have done or been here. You can be anything now, my love. Just anything. I'm doing this for you, my love. Don't be nervous. You're only seven. You'll learn everything so easily, you'll see! Papa would be proud of you. Patience. Be still Eliasz. Try to sleep."

What could have brought that memory back just then? Even without the smell of black tea and kabanosy? Perhaps it was the sense of hope mixed with fear—hope that this trip would save me or fear that it wouldn't. Leaving what I'd known behind me in search of something . . . what was it? In search of the way life ought to be.

How does anyone form a mental picture or even some subtle feeling of the way life ought to be? It must be established very early as a catalog of smells, a quality of light, and some odd assortment of sounds, whether of rain on a tin roof or of crickets in the garden. It is the archived collection of early sensorial events that coincide with the feeling of safety, well-being, and love. My first memories, though not often revisited at that time of life, as I stood on the deck of the Washington State Ferry, were of sleeping on the floor by the crackling fire in a rustic wood cottage on the edge of an ancient forest. I remember the Saints in the corner, the flickering glow of the oil lamp, and the old orange cat rubbing against my leg. I remember the trees. So many ancient trees of incredible girth. I remember their faces, their creaking voices in the wind. I remember a silence that didn't wish to be broken, except by songs of summer birds. I remember love . . . and mushrooms.

"Come with me, Ilyusha. You're mine for one more day. Let's not waste it." Babushka took the small boy's hand and started walking in her slow and careful way. They went on a silent hunt for mushrooms through the fringes of the dark primeval forest like countless times before, only this time felt different. A sadness hung like dust in a stuffy room, and the little boy felt stifled by it. They had left the usual trail behind. He didn't know where they were, but he wasn't frightened. Babushka was there. She gave him a warm sense of security, and he clung to her old country hand. It was soft and strong, with rivers running through it.

"It's good to know the forest, and the berries and mushrooms hiding in it. Here is *prawdziwek*—it's a good one, and one of the most noble of all. Many of them try to disguise themselves like the tasty, wholesome ones, but they are really poisonous and could be the last thing you ever eat. For every tasty mushroom, there are a hundred others that will kill you, so take care. Take every mushroom in your hand—examine it closely—but do not put every mushroom in your basket."

"Will these be growing in the forests around New York, Babushka?"

"I don't know, my dear joy. I don't know what grows there. But I do know that where there is a forest, there is food. You should remember how to find it. Knowing this might save your life someday. Watch me closely."

They filled the basket with fantastically shaped fungi: pipes and pagodas, bowls and balls. Babushka told the little boy their names and how best to prepare them. They continued to walk through the woods for what felt to the boy like many ages. His little feet grew tired. "Patience, Ilyusha." Finally, they came to a small wooden hut. Moss and ivy had overgrown its roof, and the boards looked sodden and unsteady. The little boy clung to Babushka.

"I want you to meet someone," she said in a hushed tone. "He might be praying, but I'll see if he can talk with us today." They circled around to the other side of the hut, and there the little boy formed one of his most vivid memories of early childhood—one that would haunt him throughout his life.

The old man sat on a stump behind the hut near a vegetable patch. He was carving a small lump of pine and murmuring to no one, or so it seemed, unless he was talking to the rabbit sitting peacefully next to him. The hermit's wild blue eyes peered over a tangled bramble of gray beard, a contradiction of derangement and incisiveness. The little boy's first valuation of the hermit was that he must be quite insane, but Babushka seemed to know him, which meant that at least he must be safe. She took the little boy, clinging reluctantly to her skirts, up close to the wild old man who looked at the child as though he was made of glass. What did he see? The boy's thoughts? His fears? His blood vessels, brain, and madly firing synapses?

"Father bless!" She bowed low in respect, kissing the old man's hand. "Our little Ilyusha leaves tomorrow for America. Will you give him a blessing for the journey, and some simple word to remember?"

The old hermit placed his sinewy hand on the little boy's head and whispered ancient-sounding words—good-sounding words like the poetry Papa used to say by the fire in winter. He looked for what felt like an eternal moment into the little boy's wide eyes, then placed two fingers on his forehead and pushed him hard! The little boy stumbled backward, shocked, looking up at Babushka for reassurance. She stood resolute with her hands clutching the basket of mushrooms—motionless—waiting. The child looked back into the hermit's wild but laughing eyes.

"It's not enough. I know what you're thinking. You think you do everything you are supposed to do. You behave well, you listen to Mama and your grandparents, you love the memory of your papa and pray for his soul. You give a little bread to the poor when they ask. Yes, of course you do, it's true. A good boy. But mind your thoughts. Mind them closely. They will take you to dark places. Though you will smile and fool yourself and the whole world into believing that you do only kindness unto others, your mind is teeming like a beehive, but not so wholesome and industrious. Be watchful. Do not nurture evil thoughts or you, my lamb, you will become evil. The appearance of goodness and goodness itself are not the same thing."

The wild old hermit pressed the small pine cross he had been carving into the little boy's hand. "Mind your thoughts, Ilyusha." He tapped the little boy's forehead with his dusty fingers to the rhythm of his words. "Mind—your—thoughts!" Then he grabbed the boy's head between his rough old hands and kissed the top of his head.

But seven is too young. A child has a profound experience at that age and is bound to lose the meaning. A simple word to remember is what Babushka had requested for her little emigrant. Something to root him to his true self and everything that he ought to be. "Mind your thoughts, Ilyusha. Mind your thoughts." What did it mean? Babushka left some of the tastiest mushrooms for the old hermit and took up the little boy's hand. It was Midsummer, and the evenings were long. They arrived home late, but not after dark. Do many young boys meet hermits in the forest, and trade mushrooms for wisdom? The little boy held this memory in his heart, though he only understood its importance too late.

2

Arrival

WHEN I CLOSE MY eyes, my head is full of voices and words. Words that others have spoken to me, words I've spoken to them, words and voices that are strangers to me, and yet they never leave: The Commentators; The Narrators; The Prosecution; The Defense; The Flatterers; and The Absurd Lunatics who just say things to shock me. It's not as though you would understand them even if you could hear them too. Do you know what I mean when I say they can "mean" without the kind of clarity of syntax one expects, at least from spoken language? They simply mean—and I know what they mean, though they are not discursive. But turn back now, if you believe that your thoughts can extend only as far as your lexis allows. There are whole universes of meaning beyond words. I've only been a tiny satellite conversing with the strange stars of a hidden galaxy firing in the synapses of my own brain. They were there—the only witnesses to my treachery.

Amid the clamor of voices, the unknown, unnamed colors, and the other things I shouldn't be seeing or hearing even with eyes open, I am searching. Always and ever searching. For what? For evidence! Evidence of the Divine. To see the Light my grandmother saw. Even some dim spark or indication that would give all matter meaning, all stories an overarching metaphor, and give all the dissonant chords of suffering their final release. I feel it must be there, even as I know that the colors exist, if only while the record is still playing Chopin on the shelf.

I must be a vain and pompous old man, trying to relate all my personal angst to that of the rest of humanity, assuming universality where maybe there is only me and my particular shipping crate of baggage. But as I draw nearer the final act of a lifetime filled with suffering, I become further convinced that most people, whether or not they recognize it as such, know what I mean when I speak of the Void. Sometimes it's merely what lies beneath the crack in a well-constructed façade, while other times it gapes like a great yawning chasm perceived only in the furthest corner of the mind's eye.

The attempt to fill this void is a common (do I dare to call it universal?) preoccupation. One person plasters over the cracks with the euphoria of experimental drugs or meditative states, while another fills the Void with a cause, or more often still with an ideal person, only awaiting the inevitable discovery that no person is large enough or perfect enough to fill it. And it is inevitable. The real impediment to sustaining worship of another human being is imperfection. The monuments we construct in veneration of our ideal people will always fall eventually, crushing us under the weight of their own failures and our own expectations. And still there looms the Void, demanding an answer, and we present our theories and arguments. Do we even believe them ourselves? But the Void must be filled with a greater *something*—something stable that we can worship—something which can be that purpose we so desperately need. In the absence of purpose, something significant enough to fill the Void, how many of us would rather reject life entirely, destroying ourselves, rather than accepting the absurdity of a purposeless life, even if the pantry is full?

In my younger days, I sought the answer to this vast emptiness in the visual arts. So many of us were doing the same at that time. In a good painting, I saw the possibility of perfection and the communication of unspeakable truths, or what one might call non-discursive knowledge. I plunged myself into becoming capable of wielding my medium with perfection and taking my place amongst the giants of artistic truth. There was a time when I felt I possessed such clarity—such a sense of meaning and mission. I entered my hallowed years at Columbia convinced of my place and purpose as an artist—a conviction that perhaps only comes from pubescent myopia and utter lack of life experience.

While classmates majoring in other more practical fields always seemed to picture me squandering my time flinging paint around with pretentious flamboyance, my long hours spent in pursuit of perfection hunched over a table in the art studio were no less painful than those of a pilgrim journeying barefoot down a dusty road strewn with sharp pebbles and overgrown with stinging plants, under the crushing weight of a wooden cross. I comforted myself in the absolute belief in this higher calling, the pride my poor immigrant mother might have felt, had she lived to see me taking my place among the luminaries of the visual arts, elevating myself socially and economically. So I continued my work ascending, so I thought, to exalted heights of understanding with each brushstroke.

We soared those heights together, Erik and I, though he filled the Void with words instead of images. He always seemed to have the right word. Back then, it felt as though we were pursuing the same vision, rejection of the coarse consumerism and material myopia of a post-war population, bent on carrying out the moral and rhetorical imperative of "nation-building." We were the original rebels who saw ourselves as ascending high above the petty stupidity, the errors of ignorance that seemed to us to saturate that epoch. With every poem, Erik seemed to edge a little closer to that dreadful precipice whose infinite mystery I was trying to paint.

Chance could not have paired more perfect roommates in that regard, though outside of our philosophical meanderings and adoption of beat generation sensibilities, we couldn't have been more different. Erik was confident, muscly, good-looking, and always seemed to have a pretty girl. He stood in stark contrast to my angular, gangly frame and taciturn disposition. He nicknamed me "Kandinsky," inspired by my chosen profession, the deep Russian roots on my mother's side, and probably my one college romance—a passionate affair with primary colors and circles. Despite our differences, our friendship seemed at the time to be one of the only real certainties in my life. How many late-night talks we had about our ideal woman, about life and ultimate meaning, topics which, at that age, frequently blurred together.

Some seasons of life are far better in retrospect. Time offers a merciful lens through which to view the past, enabling us to minimize the humiliation of rejection, the awkwardness of immaturity, and somehow magnify those moments of intense clarity when it felt like Truth was within reach and easily verbalized. In my current autumnal season of life, it is easy to mourn the loss of innocence that has led to my present state of doubt. Everything that seemed so clear and obvious when I was wearing my sparse beard and black beret—rejecting the myths of mainstream society—is now obscured in the murky twilight of experience. All certainties have become distorted in the ever-shifting sense of language to the aging psyche, and the violent churning of meaning as it crashes against the rocky shores of experience. Time and tragedy have contaminated my certainties, like the inevitable decay of all human construction. Yes, even art is temporal.

These thoughts weigh heavily on me these days. If I allow myself to dwell on what I've lost and what may or may not be still within my power to attain, a chilling fear possesses me because I catch sight of it again in the periphery of my inward vision. The beetling precipice and beyond it the limitless Void whose dimensions were never remotely explored by my artistic renderings or my own moldering collection of bankrupt ideals, and which now stretches before me more ominously than it ever has.

But there is more than one way to fill a hole. Everyone seems to approach it a little differently. One popular method is to go and sit in it yourself. The theory, I suppose, is that I am Truth and Truth is me. Truth is what I perceive it to be, what I say it is, and consolation, peace, and wellbeing is to be found in the acceptance of my own preeminence. I don't think I've ever been that self-assured, or shall I say self-deluded? Diffidence and self-consciousness have been my constant companions in life. There was never a moment when I thought I was big enough to be the answer to all the questions of the cosmos. I know myself and my own superficiality too well for that. At this point in life, I've accepted my weakness and am no longer so ashamed of it. It took time to acquire that kind of acceptance, and back then, I freely confess, I had not yet arrived.

Upon my landing at the ferry terminal, when Erik effortlessly plucked up my luggage, it was a gesture I appreciated, but one that left me feeling effeminate. I remembered that from college: the feelings of weakness, the urge to attest my masculinity. Had nothing changed since then? I fought the urge, reasoning with myself that I was no less a man for having a slight build in comparison to my friend. No, he hadn't changed much at all in those years since we had graduated and parted ways. If anything, he looked stronger, more vital, and more powerful than ever with only a few distinguished lines around the eyes and forehead. He was tan from hours spent in the sun, and his broad, straight smile glowed in contrast. He fit well into his surroundings. I noticed a lot of sunburned skin milling about the landing. I supposed that, after months of gray skies and rain, the Islanders must celebrate this season of sun.

The two-storied wooden "cottage," with its gleaming white trim, was grander than I had expected, with a vegetable garden and sprawling wooded grounds leading to the pebbly lakeshore, strewn with driftwood—or perhaps drift-trees is the better word. It seemed like a palace coming, as

I was, from my own three-hundred square foot abode in the Village. Erik led me to an upstairs bedroom, where he left me with my luggage to rest before joining him on the deck. I unpacked my bags, optimistically packed with supplies from my studio, just in case inspiration was hiding in one of those dense forests, at the bottom of the lake, or in some mossy spot under a mushroom. I wouldn't be caught unprepared.

Everything in my room was impeccably white, from the window lace to the duvet. White and fresh, and scrubbed clean. The near-constant sunshine intensified its brightness. The air in the room was cool with the suggestion of disinfectant. I set my bags down on the floor. Their very presence disfigured that airy space. I hadn't realized how dingy and worn they were until I saw them in that clean, white bedroom. I hid them underneath the bed, sitting for a moment on the edge and peering out at the view. My window overlooked the lakeshore. Sounds of the water washing rhythmically over pebbles and slapping playfully against the stacks of driftwood filled the room with wholesome, rustic music. They had the same refreshing effect on my soul. A sanitorium. That was the word. Like the ones in books where rich people suffering from tuberculosis might be sent to get well. Perhaps I would get well here, too.

When I came down, Erik stood leaning against the railing looking out over the lake wearing only faded blue canvas shorts, exposing equipment that he had kept in excellent condition over the years through the well-planned physical activity that had always come so easily to him. I had always admired, even envied, his physique and the confidence which made it all the more imposing.

We sat drinking beer and reminiscing, sending blue-gray smoke rings into the wind and watching them dissolve. We recalled the best of times from college, for those are the healthiest memories to keep. The pain of past stages of life eventually fades from memory like smoke rings in the wind, and only the ideal remains, whether it ever existed or not.

"You know, Elias, I can see it all so clearly now. Every turn, every decision leading me to this point; living in this place, breathing this air, writing about whatever inspires me in the moment. It's like a dance with every step leading to the next in some beautiful way."

"I can see why you love it here," I said.

"Some people complain about the winters, the long gray, the rain. I prefer it even to the golden summers. Fewer people around. I like the solitude. Out here, I answer to no one! I can go through the course of my day without even seeing anyone! No ugly, obtrusive, self-righteous mugs pushing in on my kingdom, no obligatory conversation with boorish, tiresome fools about just war theory, or what my poems *really* mean. I only see whom I wish to see: friends who need nothing from me, expect nothing from me, no relations—they don't even know we have a guest room they could potentially exploit! And of course, when I do want the world to see me, I get to say where and when. It's a perfectly convenient existence!"

"And Freja?"

"My goddess. We serve only ourselves, and only each other do we worship or suffer to enter our kingdom."

"Oh? What does that make me, then?"

"Court painter?" We both laughed. "I always considered myself a patron of the arts, you know. I see it as a kind of service to humanity. It doesn't hurt that you're easy to be around. An all-around good egg; you always have been."

"I've gotten a bit hard-boiled over the past couple of years, I'm afraid. It's good to get away from it all."

"Well, you can't be anything but happy here."

"You're happy, then?" I asked.

"Happy?" His laugh filled the night. "I live with a goddess in my own private paradise, leagues away from anyone who annoys me, drawing inspiration from every stone and leaf and flower, watching the sun set late at night and watching it rise again just a few hours later. I want for nothing. Wouldn't you be happy?"

"Well, when you put it like that! But I'm beginning to think that no matter where I am or what I'm doing, I'll find some reason to want things to be different. I have no memory of contentment beyond moments with my grandparents when I was too little to think things could be different. But then, I've never lived in paradise with a goddess. *Tvazho zdaróvye!*"

"Ha! Is that Polish? What does it mean?"

"It's Russian like my grandparents were. Means 'to your health.'"

"Wait now, wait now . . . I thought you were Polish!"

"I am. I'm both, I guess. At least, the village where my family is from is on the far eastern edge of Poland. Some Russian Tsar claimed it at one point. My mother's family were Russians who moved there during that period. During World War I, though, a lot of the Russian population left when the German army advanced and took over the region."

"Those Germans! We invaded Germany in 1631—we Swedes were a growing military power at that time, and the Battle of Breitenfeld was a decisive victory for us! I had relatives who were there, fighting the Imperials. We had the better tactics, you see, and slightly slicker technology—lighter cannons made a big difference for wars waged on land in those days. Anyway, we won it. We beat the Germans just north of Leipzig. In other ways, the thirty years' war didn't go quite to plan for us, but my relatives fought bravely and never retreated. So, wait, your family ran away back to Russia when the Germans came?"

"Well, no. No, my family stayed. Survived. Maybe they hid in the forest and foraged for food—I'm sure they knew how. That's just a guess, though, I really don't know how they survived. They survived the Polish-Soviet war, too, when the region became part of Poland again. During World War II, a lot of people from my village were sent to the Gulags—"

"Oh! I had a great-great-great grand something-or-other in the 1600s who was *beheaded*! His uncle was a merchant prince—a real peach of a guy. Childless. Selfish. Paranoid. Between you and me, he was probably slightly insane. He got it into his headpiece that his sister's two sons should never inherit his immense fortune. They were the closest he had to an heir. One of the brothers lost his coconut, like I said, when the old uncle tracked him down, but the other ran away to the colonies to make his own fortune. He only went back to find a wife after the uncle was dead. You see, I'm descended from crazy royalty! Also, the types who pull themselves up by their own bootstraps, as they say, escape political persecution and intrigue, and come out on top! You know, in retrospect, Ginsberg must have sensed it."

"Ginsberg?" I asked.

"You remember, that summer in the Village with the Dead-Beats between Junior and Senior year?"

"Oh, I remember. You could say I'm still living it . . . "

"Ginsberg! He must have sensed it, that I came from property and power. He never did appreciate my poems. Always said I was advertising integrity that I couldn't actually deliver. By "integrity," he probably meant poverty and obscurity. Those Beats . . . they're dead to me. Now, speaking of poverty and obscurity . . . what were you saying about the Gulag? And is it really an Archipelago?"

"Well, not in the geological sense. You should read the book, though."

"I will. Yes, I've really been meaning to. I don't read a lot of prose, you know."

"No, I know."

"But the Gulag."

"The Gulag. I don't know. There were some stories—mostly whispered so I wouldn't hear. I know the Germans and Soviets fought over our forest for years—"

"Oh, I had another great-great-great- grand- something-or-other in the 1400s who fled to a forest. Let's see, how did it go? It was political. Two important Duchies were trying to make some slick political alliance by marrying their kids to each other. The problem was, the bride was only five years old, and the groom was only six. So, the betrothal was made public at some sort of festive ceremony, and fourteen years later, they were supposed to actually marry. Well, my relative, the little boy, had fallen in love with someone else by then, probably a pretty scullery maid or something. They ran off together into the forest on the eve of the wedding and tried to set up housekeeping in a cave. Well, of course, 'treachery' was yelled on both sides because this marriage was supposed to be a done deal. Anyway, the boarhounds found them, of course, tore the scullery maid to bits, and guarded my great-great-great- grand -something-or-other until the guards came and took him back for his wedding. The ceremony was slightly delayed, I imagine. The ice sculptures no doubt had to be scrapped, but it was a successful alliance, I believe. Ha! You keep reminding me of stories! So, your forest was really something special, then?"

"Yeah, well, a lot of people seemed to think so. That's about all I know. There was just conflict after conflict over this primeval forest. All these powerful nations saw it as a resource, and the poor people living there were just caught in the middle of it all—"

"Oh, I know! I know! Absolutely caught in the middle! During the civil war, I had this old relative—too old to fight really—a farmer who ended up with the front lines establishing themselves in one of his fallow fields! So, he sees his boys getting beaten down and starting to retreat, he grabs his own musket out from under the bed and hollers, 'come on boys, follow me!' He and his old mule take up the flag and lead the charge. Slaughtered, of course, all of them. But he made his stand for his country as a poor civilian with a musket and a mule. He didn't see the fight as not concerning him, and his lack of uniform and official orders didn't slow him down! Now, what were you were saying about your family being perpetually caught between warring nations?"

"Yes, well, they survived. My grandparents and my mother somehow managed to survive. They didn't like to talk about those times to me, but I know they were hard. I'll never know the whole story, I suppose. Even how my father died. I was so young; I didn't even think to ask. I just accepted it. There's no one living now who remembers any of this."

"Okay, okay . . . now let me see if I've got this right. You are Russian, but you lived in Poland?"

"Half Russian. My mother married a Polish man. He converted to her faith, and they married in secret. His family never forgave him when they found out. They called him a Russophile, apparently, and never wanted to know me. Anyway, I grew up, at least my first seven years, hearing and speaking both Polish and Russian. I guess that's all I really needed to say to answer your question."

"I see. A mixed breed. An underdog. Bilingual. Culturally elastic."

"I guess so, but it doesn't really matter now, you know—those differences, those disagreements—Eliasz, Ilyusha, or Elias. Everyone is dead now, except me . . . and I left."

"Sure. And a good thing, too. I'm glad you're here! Here in the land of the free and the home of the Brave Viking Poet of the San Juan Islands! Did I ever tell you that I can trace my patrilineage all the way back to a Viking king?"

"I remember."

"Yes, Harald Wartooth! My grandpappy, several manly generations back. Well, anyway, welcome! And in the native tongue of my noble progenitors: *Skål!*"

We clinked glasses, then sat in silence, watching the red sun sinking into the lake.

3

The Goddess

ERIK AND I TALKED and laughed through the long twilight and well into the night. Every time I set down my glass, he descended with another splash of something I had to try. I had to try the Islay Malt, he'd said. A gentleman's drink. No, no rocks. Neat is the only way. But then there was the Irish— sweet, un-peated, oaky—but just for comparison, I had to try the bourbon. A different species. Did I taste the difference? I nodded, but I didn't.

Once my head was swimming in spirits, and I felt an invisible pressure bearing down on me, making me slide further and further down into my deck chair, vacillating between giddy laughter at nothing and overwhelming sadness, a shaft of orange light spread across the deck. To my mind, it was a golden fountain, pouring across the darkness and at its center, the shadow of an approaching form.

Elongated to incredible height in that slant of orange light, I perceived the solemn approach of a Valkyrie, come to decide my fate, yet here I was wasted. I gripped the arm of the chair, trying at once to stand and turn to greet her, but the deck was all erratic motion, the planks slipping from underneath my feet. I stumbled to my knees in front of the most beautiful bare feet I'd ever examined unintentionally at close range. Erik's booming laughter filled my head to bursting, and I recall the words "yes, bow before the goddess of beauty" whether he said them or not. I knelt there, staring at her feet, unable to stand. The deck pitched like a ship in a storm.

My eyes wouldn't go where I told them. They bounced and bobbled and refused to obey, taking in various features of the goddess before me. In the soft white cotton dress that wrapped itself around her, she was like

Venus rising out of the sea foam. When at last, my eyes dared to look at her face, it was one of marble, smooth and flawless, as though it had been chiseled and polished in ancient times. Freja looked at me, cold and emotionless, then turned her gaze to Erik, still laughing unrestrainedly in his deck chair. Her gaze then returned to me, pale gray eyes chilling me to the heart. I stared dumbly at her face, expecting something—what exactly I couldn't say. Then she silently turned her back on me and walked into the house.

"Welcome to our home," she finally said without turning to look back. Her voice was round, deep, and smooth like the resonant notes of a sad song played in the lower register of a harp. Shutting the door behind her, the golden fountain of light from which she had emerged died away into darkness. Finally, the world began to stand still again. The storm-tossed ship came into port, and all I felt was shame and nausea. I sat back in my chair, silently looking out into the dark space where I knew the lake lay still under the stars. But I wouldn't have the luxury of wallowing in my dismal performance.

"Beautiful, isn't she? Gorgeous! Pure loveliness in human form! Form, that's it! She is the very Platonic Form of Beauty—the ideal—the pattern from which the virtue of all female beauty stems! All other women seem like cheap imitations! She is the original beauty incarnate. Well, if you don't think she is just say so, you villain! Ah! Treachery! No, she's not *very beautiful*; she's *perfect*! No wonder you're a failure as an artist if you can't recognize perfect beauty when you see it! Her breasts, her lips, her hands! She's perfect! Her voice, her eyes, her mouth! The curve of her throat, the angle of her jaw, the striations of her irises . . . did you see her damn kneecaps? Even her kneecaps are perfect! What? What's that? Yes! Exactly! She's a work of art! A masterpiece! You do see it!"

I did see it. Of course I saw it. I had taken in more than I should have of her beauty and couldn't but admire it. But even in that state of utter saturation, I knew that admiring another man's wife too extensively and with too much detail is unwise. Maybe I was overly sensitive and traditional, but prudence on my part wasn't what Erik was after. He wanted fellowship in worshipping the perfections of his wife. Perhaps it was too much to drink and too late a night that caused his volatile mood. I had some vivid memories of him being an irritable drunk from our college days—particularly remembering the morning I bailed him out of prison for punching a policeman. I tried to calm him now as he threw verbal punches, which I told myself he didn't mean.

"Erik, she's beautiful! The most beautiful woman I've ever seen. You're lucky, you know, a very, very lucky man! But I've got to call it a night! You know me and spirits . . . "

Erik conceded after a lengthy monolog on the virtues of his wife's fingertips and the backs of her knees. I helped him into the house where he collapsed, face down, on a sofa, his massive arm dangling onto the floor. I found myself mentally comparing him to Odin, the Norse father-god of war and death and poetry and nearly everything else, who consumed only wine, and who, tonight, had reveled in a ritual of drunken madness and ecstasy. I was embarrassed that my visit had been the cause of this frenzy of fermented grains and regretted having had so much to drink myself.

My regret was intensified the next morning when I descended from my room with a head too heavy for my body to support and a stomach too buoyant for my body to contain as it continuously tried to float away upwards. I don't know why I had continued to drain my glass the night before. Surely there had been a point where I could have stopped. Spirits have never been a friend to me, but I used to do such things to maintain at least the appearance of a ruggedness I never possessed.

I sat down to breakfast with Erik, who seemed unaffected by the previous night's revelry. He cheerfully spread thick anchovy paste on a crusty roll, and dipped greedily into a silver egg cup, drawing forth runny orange yoke that I couldn't watch him eat. A little black coffee was all I could manage, and even that threatened to betray me.

"Where's Freja?" I asked, hoping for another chance to improve my image after the previous night's disastrous introduction.

"Oh, she won't emerge before two. Beauty rest, you know."

"Do you always stay up that late?" I asked, gulping down some aspirin tablets.

"Sure. I mean, why not, with these long summer evenings! Hey, let's go fishing!"

"Fishing?"

"You can taste the fruits of our great lake by catching your own dinner. Oh, we have coastal cutthroat trout, kokanee, largemouth bass . . . last summer, I caught a kokanee that was well over 20 inches! It's a quality population. Choice."

"Well, I haven't actually been fishing since I was seven. My dedushka took me—"

"Your what?" he laughed.

"My grandfather. He took me ice fishing a couple times when I was really young."

"What kind of a man are you, Elias? Fishing is one of the great manly pleasures for the gentleman of leisure! I go every day, rain or shine. I even wrote a poem about it. Free verse. Deep, very deep indeed. Remind me to recite it to you sometime; it's genius. Didn't make it into the last compilation, but *c'est la vie*. I can't believe you don't fish, though. Well, that's okay, just give me some time. It's good you're staying all summer. Methinks I shall make a man out of you yet!"

My tattered pride was fraying away to nothing. Not all men can be gods in this world, or even gentlemen of leisure. It wouldn't be worth being a god at all if there were no mortals over which to tower. For so many years, I had aspired to resemble my friend, even to some paltry extent. His words snagged my thin skin. I comforted myself that he still wanted my friendship, unworthy as I must have seemed in his estimation, and was willing to teach me the manly art of fishing.

4

On the Manly Art of Fishing

DISTRACTION MAY BE ONE of the most common remedies for the fear induced by the realization that one is teetering on the brink of a vast nothing. First, deny its existence, then find occupations, activities, loud, talkative friends, and hobbies to fill the time which might otherwise be spent in the dangerous *terra incognita* of serious contemplation—a state of mind where all manner of monsters dwell. The worst enemy to complacency is too much free time. And when one task becomes easy enough to do absentmindedly, another may be added. Multi-tasking may thus be considered professional avoidance of introspection.

Some tasks, however, encourage exploring one's thoughts. I had often imagined fishing to be simply an excuse to sit alone and think, at least based on my earliest memories of what constituted "fishing." One simply sits, quiet and solitary, under the pretensions of not wanting to scare the fish away, fixing one's gaze on a little piece of floating plastic because it might move, but probably won't. With hands and eyes so quietly engaged, the mind can do as it pleases. Although my father died when I was quite young, I remember him going fishing alone some early mornings when I was barely four or five. He never returned with fish. He returned happy, though; I imagine because he only wanted time to himself to think. He would bring home a bunch of wildflowers for my mother and some unusual rock or shell for me, which convinces me that it was probably us he was thinking about, at least in part.

Aside from romantic assumptions, hazy memories of wildflowers and broken shells, and the two times as a boy that my grandfather had taken me ice fishing, I had little prior knowledge or experience. Despite my inexperience and initial awkwardness, it was a great pleasure to glide across the calm lake in Erik's wood-strip canoe, which he had built with his own hands in his free time, and which he assured me was the only kind of boat for a real man. He took the stern and left me the bow. It felt as if I did the majority of the paddling while he steered, but I didn't complain. I took to the art of fishing quickly enough (how hard is it to hold a pole and watch a floating piece of plastic that might move but probably won't?) and was preparing to quietly visit one of the more pretentiously philosophical corners of my mind when Erik spoke.

"Smell that air! Drink it in like wine . . . like the heavenly draft that it is! You've been in the city far too long, living like some fungus in the shadows of skyscrapers. You look thin and peaked; it's good you came. You need to soak up some fortifying rays!"

"Well, I don't intend to have skin cancer someday—"

"Skin cancer! Faugh! Not likely!"

"Well, they say—"

"*They* don't know what the hell they're talking about! Look at the trees! Look at the flowers! Living things die without the sun! It is a warm and loving parent that embraces us, feeds us, and sustains us. Get sunshine, my pasty little friend! That's an order! See, look, even perfect goddesses can add to their perfection with a little vitamin D." He waved in the direction of the shore where a languid figure lay supine on a reclining lawn chair. "I love that bathing suit on her. I have impeccable taste in ladies' fashions, you know. Not too much ornamentation—functional but elegant and always unique. A woman with perfect breasts doesn't need too much ornamentation. She has all she requires, and too much of anything else is just gilding the proverbial lily. Not that I'd have you thinking too prolifically on the subject of my goddess's breasts."

"What? No, of course not!" I probably blushed, though I doubt whether he noticed. I was uncomfortable talking about his wife's breasts, but it was one of his favorite subjects, and he would go on shamelessly.

"Any treacherous brute who tries to steal away my goddess will know my wrath, that's damn certain."

"As well he should."

"Ha! I think all this talk of breasts is scaring all those poor puritanical trout away!"

We returned to silence. Every now and then, I would observe Freja out of the corner of my eye changing positions, loosening a string here and there to even out her careful exposure. Hers was a well-formed body, tall and willowy, I believe they call it. On the thin side, I thought, but like the artists of old whose work I admired, I preferred to draw a softer, ampler female figure. But I found myself thinking that I wouldn't mind sketching her. In fact, I thought I might enjoy it. There is something undeniably sensual about drawing the figure of an untouchable goddess, knowing that you touched her image into existence even if you will never touch the real thing. I tried and mostly succeeded in averting my gaze and focusing on that floating piece of plastic that might move, but probably wouldn't.

Eventually, it did move, beyond all probability, and I caught a large cutthroat trout—ten inches in length—which bolstered my languishing ego. Erik caught a larger one, but then we can't all be Erik. We fried them in butter and herbs that night, but Freja declined to join us, grazing instead on a meager assortment of leaves. I attempted to amend my poor first impression, engaging her in conversation.

"I see you're having salad, Freja. Are you a vegetarian?" She just stared at me. The silence was unbearable. I needed to fill it. "I was a vegetarian for two years back at Columbia. You remember, don't you Erik? You tried it too, for a while."

"I think I tried everything at Columbia," he said with a smirk.

"It was a great time! I mean, it's so heartening to know that you're living out your convictions. I never wanted to eat animals, and it felt great to say I didn't—but I got sick. My doctor told me I needed to keep a special diet including some lean meats. My health was already so . . . well, anyway, I think that's terrific what you're doing—really great." I looked at her hopefully, determined to wait out the silence this time.

"I'm not a vegetarian," she finally said flatly, looking somewhere over my left shoulder, then returning to her salad. Erik laughed, nearly choking on his bite of trout. I stopped trying and ate my dinner in silence.

Maybe it was the bad first impression or my general lack of conversational competence, but I got the feeling Freja was a woman of few words, at least in my presence. Perhaps she and Erik normally sat up late into the night talking together about poetry and philosophy, and it was only my presence that had thrown off their routine. Either way, she finished her plate of greenery and soon went back to her room, leaving us to our drinks and cigarettes on the porch.

What did she do in there, I found myself wondering? Did she read? Write? Draw? Stare into the Void and think? Was it my presence that deterred her from taking her place by Erik's side, and shyness that kept her quiet? Or perhaps a divine arrogance that didn't care to share in the presence of a mere mortal who could barely make conversation with another human, let alone a goddess. I could only guess, and Erik was filling my glass again, this time with an expensive vodka.

"You can really taste the higher quality, can't you?" I nodded, but I couldn't.

"A good day. A perfect day. I'm glad you came." Erik heaved a contented sigh.

"It *was* a good day," I agreed, "and you know, I actually had a glimmer of artistic inspiration today. I think I could paint here."

"Of course! That was bound to happen. Inspiration grows here in the flowers, it floats on the breeze like perfume, it bubbles up from the depths of the lake, and rings in the birdsong! You have to make this your summer studio. Come every year. We'll restore the old brotherhood. I can share my space in this perfect corner of the universe with a true artist and a friend! Together, we can pursue the greatness for which we are destined!"

I was flattered by my friend's nostalgic offer. I accepted without hesitation, and we agreed that I would be their perennial guest for as long as inspiration grew on his corner of the island—in other words until I died. We toasted the night into morning, gulping down burning shots of vodka. We drank to old friendships. We drank to sparkling lakes. We drank to fishing, to trees, to sun, and air. We drank to his goddess. We drank to ourselves and our destinies. Then I deposited him on the sofa unconscious, as before, and collapsed in my own bed.

. . . vodka and fishing . . . the memories played like an old movie on my eyelids, and I couldn't turn it off. That little boy who looked so familiar . . .

> Vodka never agreed with him. Dedushka said it was not for little boys anyway. The quiet old man did, however, let his darling boy help gather the roots and herbs which he would later infuse in vodka to make his own *yerofeyich*, a concoction meant to treat his stomach ulcer, ease his gout and leg cramps, and protect him from any other illnesses and afflictions to which old men become susceptible.

"The more herbs you put in, the more effective it will be." He taught the boy to identify the most desirable ones. St John's wort, yarrow, mint, wild thyme, dill, anise, the root of boronia heterophylla. "Let it be. Just leave it to infuse for two weeks or so, then you can strain it. I'll let you strain it if you like. But don't touch it until it's ready. Patience, Eliasz."

"You can put anything in vodka, really. A chili will make it twice as warm out on the ice." Their feet creaked on the thickly frozen lake. The white months are fun for children. Dedushka sat motionless on his tackle box dangling a thin line, waiting. The boy sat by him, staring at the little hole, bundled warmly, as round and red as an autumn apple. "Patience, Eliasz." Suddenly a perch flopped and floundered on the ice. Dedushka cut it up, this winter fish, dipped it quickly in the water, and rolled it in the powdery snow. It would be delicious later on.

Of course, there were other, more tempting, infusions. Sweet berry liqueurs which little boys only get to taste on Pascha, when the whole created order seemed to celebrate with that small group of Orthodox under a cathedral dome of stars, processing in the still dark morning, with dripping beeswax candles and baskets of rich, buttery kulich, eggs, and cheese. Babushka's strong, wrinkled hand clutching the boy's shoulder like a falcon's talons so as not to lose him to the darkness—*trampling down death by death*. Tired, hungry . . . drifting.

"Patience, Eliasz."

Christos Voskrese! Their voices shook the sleeping birds from the trees.

But these were just snatches of an old song I didn't need to remember. Were those memories even mine? Or were they the product of a brain swimming in spirits? Even now I sometimes feel as though these things happened to someone else, that I was simply a witness—a passive audience watching vivid childhood scenes in the cinema, the memories of some confused child born in Eastern Poland, his father's country, tenderly loved by Russian grandparents, taken away from them by a grieving mother who wanted more than anything for him to be a successful American and remember none of this. Poor Eliasz died in Poland one frigid winter, and Elias came of age in New York just when the winter crocuses were starting to push up from the cold earth, through the crust of late snow. Why was I thinking of it now—this past that was not important to remember before now? Toasting in a language I had been forbidden to speak, with a drink that only my grandfather liked. Why now? Perhaps because vodka still doesn't agree with me. I can feel it coming. It's betraying me . . . maybe not.

Vuistinu Voskrese! But me, I'm sinking lower and deeper, nearly gone. I've grown old, become someone else, and he no longer knows me . . .

I drifted into a fitful sleep.

5

Freja's Ritual

THERE ARE PROBABLY AS many reasons for drinking as there are means of bringing the alcohol onboard. Some drink because they honestly enjoy a fine wine or stout brew. Some drink as a painful duty, to avoid looking prudish or weak or unsophisticated or immature. One more ominous reason behind the urge to imbibe is to cause a dense fog to settle on the edge of that conspicuous nothing that worries the mind with its mystery. When one feels powerless to fill the Void, one might next try screening it from view. Perhaps it is what people proverbially call drinking to forget—drinking to forget to be terrified, to forget that there is this vacancy into which time is drawing us all—drinking to forget what we don't wish to remember. Everyone has their method of addressing, or not addressing, the fear that within this great nothing, there is actually something unseen and unsuspected.

My relationship with alcohol has, however, been historically capricious. While it might have lent me a brief moment of release from my inhibitions, it was followed by such a terrifying sense of physical anarchy that every time I overindulged in my younger days, the morning after would always bring with it a teetotal resolution. After those first nights of carousing with Odin, I had to beg my friend to release me to a stint of sobriety and early nights. Initially, Erik seemed surprised, rejected even, but it became evident that he was perfectly capable of carrying on his nocturnal activities without me.

At first, I was surprised in coming down to breakfast most mornings to find Erik still sleeping in his chair on the porch or laid out on the couch snoring. I particularly remember one morning when I discovered him unconscious in his beloved canoe, clinging amorously to a beaver-tail paddle.

I had initially thought that these nightly excursions into the æther were on my account—in short, an attempt to show his guest a good time. I soon revised this assumption.

In a way, it felt like I was abandoning him. For most mere mortals, drinking alone implies a state of grief or loneliness, evoking a strong sense of pathos to the outside observer. Even in a man whose very essence I venerated and sought to emulate, there was a hint of chronic melancholia in the aspect of this nightly solitary inebriation. Freja didn't share in his habit. I never saw her join him. I never came down to find more than one glass in the morning, and despite Erik's worship of his wife's beauty, I never knew them to share a bed for the night during my time with them. No, while Erik indulged in his nightly ritual, Freja engaged in a different kind of secret nocturnal activity, and one far less commonplace than swallowing shots of vodka while watching the sunset.

It happened around 4:00 a.m., in the blue-grey twilight just before dawn, on my first night without drink. First, I was roused by a light tread through the grass outside my open window, barely a whisper, but sufficient to coax me out of my light sleep. I crept to the window, lifting the lace, and looked down to see a white figure walking toward the lakeshore from the house. In that colorless obscurity of dawn light and the dreamlike state of my still-waking mind, I observed the figure, a mythical creature of the half-light, shed its robes. It was a woman beyond question . . . tall, graceful, and solemn . . . Freja.

When she reached the edge of the water, she stood on a smooth boulder surrounded by pebbles and broken shells, looked around at her congregation of water, earth, and sky, and thus began the mass. As the golden sun slid up to the horizon, her naked skin glistened like polished gold in its rays, and her hair shone like flame. A smooth and perfect nude hewn from marble and gilded with sunlight. I trembled at the sight. First, she spread wide her arms and arched her back, under the gilded dome of an adorning sky. She ran her fingers through her hair, allowing the breeze to caress it. She let the sun's long luminous fingers trip over her body in ecstasy. Was she dancing? Perhaps.

For half an hour, she posed on her rock, displaying her naked form to nature in the most bizarrely sensual dance, and suddenly I thought I understood. Hers was a frightening, dangerous act of worship—not of nature, but revealing her nakedness to the rising sun, the golden trees, the birds, and the sky that they might see her in all her glory and worship *her*.

Whether or not nature worshipped this goddess as she conducted her sunrise ceremony was unimportant, for I could see that she was worshipping herself—her own youthful beauty, her own perfect form. That was enough. When the rite concluded, Freja stepped solemnly from her stone alter, cheeks flushed, perhaps with the exhilaration of her own beauty, and slowly, quietly, she returned to the cottage, her white robe trailing behind her from her fingertips.

How can I describe what I felt? I sat awake in my room for the remainder of those small hours of morning ruminating on what I'd seen, trying to explain it to myself, trying to understand my own response to it. I felt feverish with pleasure, but a massive pang of guilt soon overpowered me—guilt for having allowed myself to watch her, my friend's wife, and a woman who was not for me, exposing her radiance in the confidence that she was safe from prying eyes.

Mind your thoughts, Eliasz. Mind—your—thoughts.

Worse still, I had seen something secret and sacred and terrifying. I had seen a goddess shed her robes and saw that underneath she was indeed flawless, ideal Beauty—perhaps the mother of all beauty—the daughter of earth and sky. She had been aptly named.

In a way, I envied my friend, the manly equivalent to this goddess, who could call her his own, look on her beauty without shame, feel her warmth and embrace, fall asleep in her arms and make love with her in the warm breeze of midsummer. I thought at first what a lucky man he was. But Erik wasn't lucky. He was Odin—the father of gods. They were the only two people on earth who could look on one another's full majesty without being consumed by flame and struck dead by the terrible sight. It was only by some unknown grace that I escaped that fate.

That morning as I sat alone in all my guilt, reflecting on what I'd seen, I resolved that if I were roused in the night again, I wouldn't watch her, and from that point on, I would be a protector of all that was precious to my friend. But mortal flesh is weak, and I watched her every night. Her dance was for nature, but wasn't I part of the natural world as well? Why shouldn't I look and worship along with the birds and lake and sky? I knew I didn't really want to possess her. She was his. I only wanted to draw her.

The appearance of goodness and goodness itself are not the same thing.
A good mushroom hunter knows the difference.

6

A Midsummer Night's Mare

COVER IT, FILL IT, ignore it—there are as many ways to calm our fears of the Void and of personal annihilation as there are people in the world. One useful method is ever and always bombarding the mind and body with novel experiences. As long as there is something new to dazzle the senses, there is little need to heed the approach of an ancient and timeless abyss. Experience can be a drug in which we lose ourselves—lose, for a moment, our fear. It may be the hard, loud rush of wind that blasts the face and cuts through to the very bone as one leaps from an airplane, watching the end of one's universe approach, secure in the knowledge that one always holds the key to salvation in the form of a parachute. In this sense, one spits into the faceless abyss, claiming ultimate sovereignty over the tiny flame of life, holding it in one's own hands. More subtly, it may be the soaring of the emotions upon hearing a new piece of music, or reading a new poem, or even of kneading, baking, and eating, a warm, crusty cottage loaf while raindrops slither down the windowpanes. The darkness needn't be paid too much heed while there is still beauty and warm bread. Indeed, why give in to gloomy thoughts when midsummer daisies are waving in the breeze?

The summer solstice of 1974 arrived with splendor and gaiety in all her flowery garb. In every corner of the garden the simple faces of daisies smiled, nodding gently, humming with insects. The long-awaited day had come, and Erik rushed busily around the cottage and the garden adding last-minute touches to the picnic offerings and the towering, phallic may-pole twined with yellow and white daisies. This was his favorite day of the year—a day when he felt his Swedish roots more intensely than ever. Erik was proud of his origins, intensely interested in genealogy, and despite never having set foot on the native shore of his ancestors, he considered himself no less a Swede, and this was his day. Since taking up residence in this secluded corner of the world, he had annually opened his home to a select group of friends and acquaintances—most either beautiful or intellectual—for a midsummer garden party.

Erik had been up with the birds for the first time that summer, erecting and decorating his maypole, receiving dishes from caterers, and completing his own culinary contribution of pickled herring, the creation of which he said couldn't be outsourced. His labors this year had not been in vain. The overall effect was simple, yet breathtaking and filled me with a sense of warm nostalgia, despite the newness of the experience for me. It was like the embodiment of a half-forgotten dream, as though every bitter-sweet longing I had ever felt, every sensation of Sehnsucht—that homesickness for a place, as yet, unexperienced—was answered in the blithe and uncomplicated freshness of this Swedish/American midsummer.

Erik rushed around, neurotically adjusting and rearranging the buffet table, cursing when he burnt his hand on a chafing dish for the third time that morning, and refusing any help. I kept my distance, sitting just out of range of his oaths, in the quiet shade of a Douglas fir. I stared long at the intricately patterned jumping legs of a grasshopper some feet away from me, and I became conscious of a lightness of heart that I hadn't felt since early childhood. There is a brief period in life when experiences are fresh, emotions are straightforward, longings are innocent, and joy is untainted by sad memories. In that quiet midsummer moment, I felt a fleeting return to all that I had given up for lost—the wholesome goodness and simplicity that I thought had died with my father on a midsummer day, not unlike this one.

> That summer evening was iconically sweet as the little boy squatted on his heels in the garden. Babushka had given him permission to capture insects in the cabbage bed if he promised to be gentle with them. "There are enough amputees in this village already," Babushka had said. He hopped like an insect himself, on his haunches, from row to row, plucking little green bugs and dropping them in a red plastic bucket with a hollow plunk. He stretched a handkerchief over the top of the bucket, securing it with a piece of twine to keep the insects inside. Papa would be home soon, and they would walk together into the forest to let the insects go free.

"We don't kill or injure living things needlessly, Eliasz. Insects are not malicious—only hungry. Let's be generous by showing them a better place for a meal than our garden."

He heard the heavy tread of boots coming up to the cottage. Not Papa's. Not a man he recognized. An official of some sort. He knocked forcefully on the door, with such urgency that Eliasz trembled. He didn't hear distinct words from inside the cottage— only intonations. The low baritone rumble of the visitor's voice. A gasp from Babushka. Disconsolate sobs that sounded like Mama, but different from any sound he had ever heard from her before. A heavy feeling came over the little boy as he realized he would be taking his bucket into the forest alone.

The sad old song of memory—the dances and the dirges—the dissonant phrases. Why did they keep returning here and now? Why would it not disappear with him—with them? Was it the grasshopper? The season? Why was it that no one had thought to teach me how to grieve back then? That moment—that dreaded verse—came into Erik's garden like something that had happened to someone else, but that I had observed from a distance. It was only with the dawning of adulthood that I could acknowledge all that I had lost that day, and when at last, I could acknowledge it, then the tears came. Little though I understood it at the time, it had been that summer day in the garden, with my bucket of insects, when first I'd caught a glimpse of the Void opening its jaws before me, and I felt afraid. It had always been there, but I had only just noticed it. The terror I felt in that moment would follow me to my Greenwich loft, to my faded chartreuse armchair, to that dark moment when I considered ending it all.

But all the terror and angst that had previously gripped me as I stood upon the precipice of annihilation, contemplating that ultimate leap, felt finally soothed in the warm embrace of the sun and the cheerful simplicity of flowers dancing in the breeze. Perhaps it was a mere palliative, but I let those happy feelings linger as long as they pleased, basking in them like a cat who has discovered the sunniest spot in the room and claimed it as his own, stretching out, belly up, eyes closed in ecstasy. It doesn't matter that the sun will eventually move. It's in this exact spot at this exact moment, and so is he.

I remember feeling so poignantly that I was at the beginning of something. But it was not a beginning, much as it felt like one. Why is it so easy to confuse beginnings and endings? They merge together, confusing me as to where I've started, where I'm going, and where I've been. How easy to impose chronology on my life, but how difficult to interpret it under such a construct when my past, present, and future would all one day converge under a fir tree, much like this one in the midsummer garden. There I sat, in the sunset of my innocence, comfortable in the belief that I was basking in a glorious sunrise.

Like a trembling dewdrop on the gossamer thread of a spider's web, the slightest disturbance causes the gleaming orb of solitary reflection to fall, crashing aground like it had never been. The not-unexpected arrival of a few guests and Freja's grand entrance into the garden chased away these reflections, brought me back into the world, and I remembered where I was—what I was.

Freja seemed to float on the breeze in a thin, white cotton dress. It clung to her like a thing enamored and revealed less than subtle hints of the form underneath when the sun shone through it. She was a feast for the eyes and seemed to take pleasure in every hungry glance she received.

The small party consisted of two other young, attractive, and fashionable women—friends of Freja's visiting from Los Angeles—and a handful of young intellectuals and aspiring writers with whom Erik enjoyed considerable respect and seniority having actually published a reasonably well-received volume of poetry a few years ago. There were also two photographers present, a seasoned, grey-bearded bear of a man and his apprentice, a small, unassuming young woman in her late-twenties. The group dynamic established itself quickly. Freja and her friends kept to themselves, and Erik expanded with an extra measure of impressiveness in the company of his unpublished friends, with whom I stood quietly listening for some time as Erik held court.

Erik had always possessed this certain impulsiveness that only added to his overall charm. His ambitions were so lofty and his manner so genuine that his listener might be easily swept up in his dreams and carried along the raging current of his goals. His infectious enthusiasm gave the impression that he was a genius on the brink of realizing his greatness. A more cynical soul might have thought he was well-suited to snake-oil salesmanship, but for myself and the impressionable young scholars with whom I stood, there was little doubt that he would be one of the great men of letters in our generation. One moment he was waxing eloquent on the topic of semiology, another on "Burkology" or some other contemporary rhetorician whose work he critiqued harshly enough to seem superior to them, but with sufficient generosity to avoid the appearance of any unsightly arrogance. Erik was a tidal wave, sweeping us into his own turbulent world, tossing us effortlessly from one concept to another. He always had a new idea—a new plan for greatness.

When I grew weary of listening to rarified literary banter and having nothing to say myself, I attempted to talk shop with the photographers. This I did to the meager extent that I could without appearing utterly ignorant of the photographic arts. Or coming off as snobbish for that matter considering, as I did, photography to be an artistic expression far inferior to painting.

I talked at length with the young apprentice, whose worthy name I won't further mar by stating here, for indeed, she's suffered enough on my account. She spoke so eloquently and passionately of her art that, under the influence of her contagious zeal, I could begin to admit my own medium to find a genuine rival in the work of a talented photographer. I remember her eager enthusiasm, so youthful and zealous, but eloquent as she preached the merits of her art.

"As you and I both know," she said with modest authority, "the untrained eye judges a work of art by how realistic it is and, forgive me, but the photographer will win this competition every time."

"Not a competition worth winning. You can have the untrained judges' acclaim!" I said with pompous confidence that I felt sure was convincing.

"No, but even that is based on an untrained assumption. To think that the photographer simply points the camera and—click—there's the picture! There's the art! And they know it's art because it looks like something they've seen and thought beautiful."

"You think photography can transcend the obvious, then? Become truly Art, and not just an exact reproduction of the surface of reality?"

"Of course! The photographer becomes an artist when she's not content with what's obvious—what's literal and ready-made for her on the surface of things. She will use her artistic judgment in choosing her point of view, the point and degree of focus. She may use a filter or different lighting and make certain decisions in developing her film that make striking differences to the meaning of the photograph. In this way, she manipulates not only optical but conceptual perception. She looks for what emotion the scene may evoke in her mind and works to capture the unexpected truth hidden within the simple facts, often by obscuring those very facts so that the truth may come forward into the light."

"But emotion and hidden truth is so obviously the realm of painting," I argued. "How much can you really obscure reality in a photograph without making it simply a bad photograph? Reality is what photography does best!"

"No, it's really not! By dipping below the surface of what's obvious, and bringing forward her own vision of truth, the photographer can address emotion just as poignantly as the painter. She can make the viewer feel as if he has left the everyday world and entered into a richer and more sensitive realm, which may seem disturbing, or tragic, or even sacred. No, no, I'm sorry, but we're chasing after the same secrets, only with a different medium."

"And what secret, tragic, and sacred truths do you intend to find here today, in this little garden party, with these particular human specimens?" I probed. I was enjoying her zeal and didn't want her to stop.

"Ah, now, you should know it's not for the artist to spell it out for you that way. You'll see the pictures, no doubt. Erik commissions these every year, and I've decided this year is my last, so I'm not holding back."

"Intriguing."

"I hope so. When you do see my photos, I'm sure you'll see what truth is hiding here. It may take some time. Any good piece of art requires quality time to impart its effect, but when, at last, you've seen it, you will never be the same again. It will be as though you have emerged from the chrysalis of your own confined perception." She said this with eyes widened and brows raised in an exaggerated expression of what I took to be mock seriousness. I laughed, if only because I believed she wanted me to.

"You seem to have summed me up rather quickly. Are you sure my perception is so limited?" I pursued.

"Of course it is!" she laughed. "But don't be afraid. It's startling at first, out in the cold open air," she said, sinking into a whisper most enigmatic, with that same joking expression, "but then you'll fly."

"Will I?" I answered, matching her whisper.

"Oh, I'm sure you will! Well, probably. I don't know you, after all, but I have a good feeling about your prospects!" We both laughed. She laughed because she knew exactly what she meant, and I because I had absolutely no idea, but laughing felt right in the moment.

We all sat on a checkered cloth spread over the grass and enjoyed the picnic of Erik's pickled herrings, strawberries, buttered new potatoes, and steak. Schnapps was drunk, naughty songs were sung, and many happy toasts were made, all of which was documented by the photographers who, between bites, snapped away at the picturesque scene in the natural light. I began to notice that they were focusing the majority of their attention on Freja, for she was the reason they were invited.

As the evening wore on, all the tipsy activity escalated in silliness as the three self-conscious beauties, Freja and her friends, affected wistful sighs and attitudes while making clumsy daisy chains in the dappled light that fell on the grass while the photographers kept snapping from every possible angle and ridiculous position. I was bored. Bored with all this vanity and being thus extricated from the sweet influence of my young apologist, I returned to my belief that there is something very crude and vulgar about photography. One may capture a moment in all precision, but it is nothing compared to the intimacy of painting the truth of a moment with your hands. I muttered these opinions in my most pretentious tone. Erik didn't seem to share my feelings but rather threw out suggestions for different poses and angles. A little more shoulder. Less pout. From worm's eye view. From the tree. It began to dawn on me that the midsummer picnic was merely an excuse to photograph his wife in the beauty of their garden and the golden sunlight using the colored film that was steadily growing in demand at that time.

"There, that's perfect. Just the right balance of innocence and seduction. You have to have both, you know. Enough innocence to ensure the seduction isn't cheap, and enough seduction to ensure the innocence isn't sexless. Freja doesn't even have to try. It's those idiot friends of hers who can't get it right." Erik said, a little too loud. They all turned their platinum blond heads in our direction.

"Oh . . . well, they're all lovely, though." I tried to make up for Erik's less than generous assessment of his wife's friends, a naïve gesture that I would learn to regret.

"But which of us do you think is prettiest?" One of Freja's friends called over to me, with a devious smile.

"Yes, who does the painter prefer?"

"Would you paint me?"

"Which of us would you like to paint the most?"

"You have to choose. You have to now!"

"Oh, no! Don't ask me that! I wouldn't—I mean, I couldn't—" I blushed and looked frantically at Erik, who looked back at me with expectant amusement, arms folded across his chest. He wouldn't be rescuing me.

"No, no, don't be shy! Which of us is most beautiful to your artistic eye?" Freja's friends looked at me with the teasing smiles of grammar-school flirts, while Freja herself regarded me silently with the cool self-confidence of a woman who is in no doubt of her own superiority in the eyes of any man who dares to look.

While I knew that my hostess expected her perfections to be sung, it felt like crossing a line to state a preference for my friend's wife so publicly. However, I couldn't comfortably choose one of her friends because even worse than showing an unseemly partiality for a married woman would have been humiliating my hostess in front of her friends. Three beautiful women stood before me, awaiting my judgment, and I couldn't decide. My efforts at diplomacy were failing.

How differently I would have answered if given a chance today to re-live this scene—and I *have* relived it countless times in my imagination. I picture myself offering some eloquent, jaw-dropping condemnation of the objectification of women, if not all human beings, and even all living creatures! I imagine myself telling them off right soundly for caring so much about nothing. However, at that time, I still accepted, albeit unconsciously, the rightness of the status quo. I was still caught in the snare of my genera-tion, in the snare of the ages, the tragedy of womankind—no, of human-ity—throughout the millennia: seen not for themselves but for the pleasure and satisfaction they can give. Women, these precious human creatures, grasped, exploited, and devoured, inheriting and dare I say accepting the injunction generation after generation to be young and beautiful, for what better virtues can a woman possess? To attract attention, to inspire worship, to preserve the fading flower of youth as long as possible before raising up the next generation fully prepared to fall prey to the same fate: to be used up and consumed like a pretty iced tea cake.

But we're all like this. Aren't we? Captive to the invisible boundaries and expectations we're never told that we're meant to abide by, yet sure enough, we do. We learn our parts, we men and women, and play them only too well, more often than not. And where does it lead us? To become selfish, simplistic, hierarchical, controlling, irrational, delusional, fright-ened, noisy, starving souls—fragile wood shavings, curling around our own internal emptiness—perpetually failing to understand ourselves and each other, perpetually trying not to need each other, and perpetually terrified by our self-imposed isolation. Learning to pile on distraction after distraction from our wounded state of being, continuously playing the same scenes with the same roles, only to realize it was all a diversion when the curtain drops. Only to realize we've been played by history like a fiddle—swept on the current of a song whose notes should never have been sounded—a song that is the shame of humanity.

But these are all just words. I have so many of them now—now that it's too late. I had no words for all of this back then. I knew—how could I not—that it was wrong. I knew no better way out in those self-conscious days than to play the part that was given to me. The company grew impatient with my hesitation.

"You must have an opinion," one of them claimed. "The one of us you choose will reward you with a kiss, how does that sound?" The others nodded their tipsy consent to this proposal, and I panicked.

Amid my frantic deliberation, a solution came to me. Had I been allowed more time to think about its possible repercussions, I might have thought better of it, but at that moment, it seemed the only way to clear myself of wrongdoing (woe to my ignorance). I looked past the three towering beauties to the junior photographer. I hadn't studied her in that way, but I looked at her then as a way out. Yes, she was attractive in an unorthodox way. Her unremarkable clothes hid her form like a secret, and her face was beautiful in its unstudied humanity. She was not a goddess. She was a fully mortal person. Encountering her wasn't a flat, aesthetic experience. She was a person full of nuance and dimension. Not a perilously fair undying soul, but the kind one learns to love and respect for her substance. Her conversation gave unmistakable evidence of a deep and questioning soul, with signs of real feeling written on her face like a poem and thrilling in her voice like a song. Those few minutes of conversation with her convinced me that her prettiness deepened into beauty by the discovery of real substance of mind and intellect. I liked her best of all, and I pronounced my honest judgment as confidently as possible.

Silence.

A pregnant silence followed for longer than was comfortable, then Freja's friends laughed unkindly at the audacity of voting for someone who wasn't on the ballot. I felt instant regret as the young photographer looked at the ground humiliated. Upon their sarcastic urging, she kissed my cheek then excused herself to the house.

Erik finally rescued the dangling spirit of the party by leading us in a rousing drinking song. The topic changed, to my relief, and no one looked at me anymore . . . except for Freja. Her penetrating stare never seemed to leave me that night. Her gaze was like a scimitar savagely slicing through me. It was a stare unconcealed and unapologetic—a relentless, chill conflagration of resentment whose fingers grasped the throat of my self-possession and squeezed.

Erik's eyes, however, didn't meet mine for the remainder of the party. I could only guess that I had given the wrong answer, and this was a figurative calm before the storm of his discontent, which would break loose when the company disbursed. I had only to wait and observe anxiously as he lost himself to drink.

Patience, Eliasz.

7

The Impending Storm

THE SUN HAD BOTH set and risen again when the last intoxicated guest departed. Freja went directly to her bed, and Erik finally gripped my shoulder roughly.

"Let's take the boat out." He swayed a little but seemed able to hold a paddle. There was no refusing him.

We pushed away from the shore, gliding out onto the clear, glassy lake, the surface of which flamed with early morning mist. The only sound for some time was water lapping against the sides of the canoe, punctuated only by birdsong echoing through the morning air. I waited uneasily for Erik to speak. At length, he did.

"So, it's been a few hours now. Have you thought up an answer yet? Revised your word choices? Finessed your rhetoric? Convinced your own mind that the answer is true?" We stopped paddling in the middle of the lake. I stared at him uncomprehendingly.

"Answer?" I asked in an involuntary whisper. "I need to hear the question first." Erik shook his head. His expression fluctuated from bewilderment to anger to pity and back again in mere seconds.

"Why? Why did you . . . what . . . whatever could have possessed you? It was a foolish thing! *Foolish*, Elias! A *treacherous* thing!"

"I was trying . . . I wanted to do the *right* thing. I thought I had."

"In what alternate reality?" Erik exploded, the boom of his voice echoing across the lake and setting the feathered inhabitants of a bush to flight. "*I* can forgive you. *I* can laugh at the absurdity, pity the stupidity. But why would you risk . . . why would you provoke *her* like that?"

"I only wanted to show your wife the kind of respect she deserves. I didn't want to disrespect her or you by basically making her into some sort of . . . I don't know . . . an art-thing! Or humiliate her by preferring one of her friends. For the love of all that's holy, Erik! She's your wife! I couldn't just . . . and in front of your company . . . and that stupid kiss! What was I supposed to do?" Erik's features softened toward me as, I imagine, he pictured his wife kissing another man, even one as unthreatening as myself. "Don't punish me for protecting what's yours. My intentions were pure." I sat in silence before the judge, waiting for him to hand down his verdict.

"No. I suppose I should thank you for that. So, you didn't actually think that fat little girl was . . . ha! No, how could you? How could anyone? Next to Freja, she's . . . " He shuddered. I was offended and felt moved to defend her, however immaturely. How I hate the things I've said and worse the things I've thought!

"She's pretty, in a normal, natural sense," I said. "She's a girl from my stratum—the stratum of ordinary mortals! I can appreciate and relate to her. You know what I am . . . you know what I'm *not*! Freja . . . she's a goddess. What's more, she's *your* goddess!" Erik examined my face for a moment, then smiled grimly.

"Of course. I understand you now. I see your intentions, I do, and don't think I'm not grateful. You're a good person—a good friend. Diplomatic. A little naïve. What you don't seem to realize is that you've drifted into uncharted waters. I don't envy you. I wish I could forecast what lies ahead and give you some reassurance. But the truth is that things like this simply don't happen. I can't predict the outcome. You may be in for a storm, and I doubt there's anything I can do to smooth the waters. Freja . . . she's . . ." He never finished, but he didn't need to. I understood his meaning well enough to brace myself. I had, in her estimation, betrayed her most basic maxim: all praise, honor, and worship belong to the goddess of beauty. All other allegiances or proprieties come second to upholding the first maxim.

We sank back into a heavy silence. I watched glistening drops fall rhythmically from my beavertail onto the smooth surface of the lake, the ripples growing and spreading ever outward. The birdsong continued to ring through the woods, directionless as my future.

Patience, Eliasz.

8

The Passerby

I WENT TO BED that early morning roiling in the uncertainty of my future after the conversation with Erik on the lake. I simply couldn't imagine what lay ahead, but my sleep was disturbed by all sorts of bizarre possibilities. In one half-sleeping dream, I imagined myself standing in the kitchen the next morning, toasting a bagel. Freja came up behind me and detached my head from my body with a bread knife, and none too quickly. My body jolted involuntarily, waking me to the reality of a new day in which seemingly anything could happen.

I came down finally around noon, fearing the worst, but everything seemed perfectly normal. When I saw Freja, she treated me with the same indifference as usual, but no malice . . . or dull bread knives. Perhaps I'd let myself worry for no reason. Perhaps Freja wasn't as vindictive as all that. Nothing much seemed amiss at all. Perhaps I had been pardoned? Or perhaps Erik and I had done Freja a gross injustice by fearing some form of retribution for my sin against her beauty. I still stepped lightly, but her behavior gave me some small hope that all might be forgiven.

A little later that week, I plucked up the courage to wander into town and find the one I felt truly deserved an apology: the young apprentice photographer from the midsummer party. I didn't know what I would say. I thought I should somehow make amends for the cruel remarks to which my actions of self-preservation had exposed her. I knew I had embarrassed her, exposed her to ridicule, even made her into an "art-thing" the same way I had been avoiding with Freja. When I stopped by the studio of her mentor, the bearded silver bear, he directed me to a coffee shop where she often went to take pictures in the afternoon. I found her there, sitting outside with an empty cup, talking most gravely to a dachshund tied to a street sign before taking a picture of it. When she noticed me, she didn't look surprised to see me but just smiled.

"May I join you?" I asked. She looked around us suspiciously, as if I had asked her to help me rob a bank, then motioned for me to sit.

"Finding hidden truth in a wiener dog?" I asked.

"Yes, but don't call him that. He doesn't like it."

"Oh, okay. But let's hear more about this morning's hidden truth you've discovered." I pulled my chair an inch closer.

"Innocence, chiefly. Dogs are quite innocent. Animals, in general, are innocent, but I think dogs are particularly so. They're so much better at being people than humans are."

"Ha! What does that mean?"

"Oh, you know! Brave, loyal, long-suffering, generous, unprejudiced, loving . . . all the things we ought to be but usually aren't. The things that come naturally to us as children but are so often forgotten as adults."

"Well, that's not how I'd describe your average junkyard pitbull."

"Oh, now don't be unjust. It's not their fault, you know, poor things. We've done that to them for our own purposes. Made them a means to an end like we've done with everything else . . . and with each other . . . " She gave me a knowing look. I smiled apologetically, accepting the implied reproach as well-deserved.

"I'm still not sure I'd so freely glorify an animal with a penchant for eating its own feces. Humans seem to be a little better at personhood in that department," I joked, instantly regretting my use of the word "feces" and groaning inwardly.

"Well, sure, a human behaving that way would be called 'insane.' But it's the insane ones, the fools, who always get the best, most potent lines in Shakespeare, in Dostoyevsky. In fact, you might say they're stark raving sane where it counts."

"How can I possibly argue with these venerable literary titans? I'll give you that truth often stumbles from the mouths of toddlers and long-eared equids—" (was I trying to sound like Erik? I certainly didn't sound like myself!) "—but given a choice, I think I'd prefer a cat."

" . . . oh . . . " she said cryptically after a brief pause.

"Oh?" I pursued. "Care to elaborate?"

"Oh. Just oh. You told me something intimate and profound that tells me more about yourself than you seem to realize, and I'm afraid saying anything else will hurt your feelings."

"Oh, go on. Hurt my feelings. Flay me alive, but don't keep me in suspense."

"You're sure?"

"How can I resist your analysis of my cat preference? You've made it too mysterious."

"Okay. Well, you say you prefer cats: independent, solitary, individualistic, moody, unpredictable, absent fathers (yes, that at least is predictable except in the case of lions), users of the people and other creatures around them for their own capricious desires. They never quite trust. They never quite love. One moment they can't get enough of your affection, and the next, they're swiping at you as you walk past. I love cats, don't misunderstand me. But I would say that inherent to your cat preference, either you identify with some or all of these traits, or you at least find these characteristics truer to the human condition, and thus more relatable—which would be correct. Most humans, especially in our geographical locale, are far more like cats than dogs. We're bent almost to breaking point away from all that we could be to the point where the bravery, loyalty, and generosity of dogs seems naïve—unsophisticated—the values of some lower being yet to learn the real ways of this world. In short, it tells me you're wounded."

"Wounded? How? By whom?"

"You needn't be quite so literal about it. I mean, I suppose maybe you were bullied. Maybe your brother or your cousin picked on you and made you grow up feeling stupid and unwanted. Maybe your father left when you were young. Maybe you tell yourself that you choose solitude because it's your nature, but in reality, you're lonely and haunted because you're afraid of other people. Afraid that they will leave you or find you repulsive. Most people have been wounded by the people they love and admire at some point. We get over that, eventually. But the real wounds, the deep wounds, are self-inflicted. Do you keep a cat?"

"No, I don't believe in pet ownership."

"Interesting."

"But for argument's sake, suppose I have wounded myself. Why would I have done that, to begin with, and what kind of wound are we talking about?"

"No one can injure us more than we can ourselves, and we usually don't notice until we're in critical condition."

"Supposing I am in critical condition. How would you go about diagnosing me?" I asked.

"I can't do that. Your wounds are for you to discover, not me. It could be so many things. I wouldn't pretend to know. I only say you're wounded because we all are—some more than others. Some people are wounded through wanting and loving the wrong things, though maybe more often from not loving enough. I'm talking about disorders of the soul."

"And you think you can be wounded without knowing it?"

"Of course! Aren't our whole lives just one long rehab session? Trying to return to that time before we felt the weight of a growing soul within us? The wounds we sustain as we grow can be like scratches and snags on a hike that you only notice hours later and can't remember when or how they happened. You never know you have these wounds until you actually find evidence of them. Those are quicker to heal because they're on the surface. Of course, there is also the possibility of profound illness, like cancer you don't discover until it's quite advanced. Those are dangerous situations and scary, but better to search your soul and find that sort of thing early on, before the damage is too severe.

"Wow . . . "

"What?"

"This just isn't the conversation I was expecting at all. I thought I'd come down here and have a nice chat about the weather or coffee or popular music, maybe apologize for being an ass last night, and now I have stage-four soul-cancer! Are you even capable of small talk?" I wanted to sound witty. I wanted to be Erik. I tried to sound unfazed by her words.

"Time is precious. Why waste it on trivialities?"

"So, I suppose you wouldn't have enough time for a walk with me? Too trivial?" I ventured.

"Not necessarily. Walks in the woods are never a waste of time. We should always make time for the trees."

"A deep, meaningful walk in the woods then—will you come?"

"Of course! Just let me say my farewells to Günther."

"Who?"

"The wiener dog, as you call him. And by the way, he's still waiting for your apology." We both laughed, and she packed up her camera.

We passed beyond the main street and walked silently into a dense tangle of evergreen that dappled the secluded path with shifting, undulating patches of sunlight. When the trail narrowed, she led the way ahead, and the lights played in her hair, picking up strands of red and gold. She smelled like the woods, a delicious incense of pine and sunshine, and touched each tree she passed it as if greeting an old friend. We stopped for a moment to listen to the birds, sitting on a fallen log that was covered thickly in the shaggy moss that clung to anything that held still long enough. We watched the slow, gentle rhythm of the tide on the pebbly shore of a shallow, crescent-shaped inlet. We observed as the waters slowly receded, leaving behind bits of shells and sand dollars, stained green with algae.

"I'm really sorry . . . " I finally stammered.

"Please . . . " she began, holding up a hand, but never finished.

"I know it can't change what happened last night, but please believe that I didn't mean to . . . I mean, it wasn't my intention to humiliate you or make you seem like . . . I don't know, like something cheap, I guess. In all honesty, though . . . I did mean what I said."

"I was afraid you might," she said without taking her eyes off the water.

"Why?"

"You still don't understand. It's not that you used me, you know. They put you in an awkward position. People say silly things when they don't have time to think."

"What should I have said?"

"It'll come to you someday. I promise you'll think about it years from now. It'll come in those hours—you know the ones. The hours that are so late they're early. When time seems to stop yet seems never to end. When sleep won't come. When I'm nothing but an old man's memory. It'll probably come to you then when you can't distinguish your past from your future because it all crowds into your present, and you'll think you're going mad."

I perceived that she was talking poetry, which I didn't understand at all, but I liked how it sounded as she said it. She reached for my hand, which she held so naturally as though we were children. The kingfisher laughed from his branch then plunged through water's surface as though breaking into another dimension. I felt it was my turn to say something. But what?

"Well, yes, I'm sure I'll think of you a great deal in the days to come, but I hope I see you again and arrive at a better answer before I'm an old man with insomnia." Why did I try so hard to sound clever? It didn't work.

"I won't be seeing you again, I don't think," she said, still keeping her eyes on the waves as they churned up smooth rocks, seaweed, and traces of perished sea life.

"Why not?"

"You'll understand soon enough. Ask to see my pictures next year, if you remember. Give them some quality time. You'll have to figure them out for yourself—I won't be there to help. I hope they can help you find the truth but be careful with it once you've found it. And . . . don't judge them too harshly."

"The pictures?"

"Your friends."

"I just . . . I don't understand you at all. Are you going somewhere?"

"Of course. I always was. Please don't blame yourself too much. What you said at the garden party was really just the last nail in a coffin I had already made for myself this summer. I knew what I was doing, though why I was doing it was less certain," she said, finally looking at my face. "I've been wondering what it was for, you know. Maybe it was for you."

I just looked at her. Her mouth smiled, but her eyes cried. I should have wiped her tears. Why didn't I? I didn't understand. I didn't understand anything then.

Finally, she embraced me like a warm breeze, as if we had been old friends seeing each other for the last time. I felt her tears on my neck as I held her, my mind swarming with such confusion, such questions, but no words—not one. It would have been the wrong word anyway. And then she left me there alone.

I often think of my life in terms of things I regret having done. Only with my mysterious photographer, that eloquent soul who was so bad at small-talk, do I regret all the things I didn't do—didn't say—but I didn't understand, and she never told me. No one told me, beyond subtle warnings and innuendos too opaque to make sense except in retrospect. I understood far too late. Perhaps I could have found her again, this passerby who tried to help me before I knew I needed help. I dearly wish I had—my young apologist for the art of photography, who smelled of pine and sunshine. Her embrace made the Void feel small and far away for a moment. She forgave me my shallow weakness and knew me better than I knew myself. She summed me up so quickly while I imagined myself so complex. I sometimes wish I had painted her face—so open and sincere, but I didn't. She left me by the shore, speechless as the empty shells that shattered under the weight of my feet. I never saw her face again, except as an old man's memory.

9

Beauty

I DIDN'T SEE MUCH of Freja after Midsummer's Eve. I didn't regret it.
I enjoyed the calm while keeping a weather eye open for the breaking
storm Erik had forecasted. I felt the sky could turn dark at any moment.
Whenever I found myself alone by the lake with my easel, I somehow felt
that her grey eyes, like storm clouds, were fixed on me from some secret place. Before the night of the midsummer garden party, I had hardly
been worth her notice. I was just another man who's worship she never
doubted possessing. In the days following, I was baffled by her treatment
of me when our paths did cross, as they had to under the same roof. She
didn't speak to me; she didn't need to. She fixed me in her unapologetic
gaze and smiled—a smile without humor, and without clear intention.
There are worlds within some women's smiles, but within Freja's, there
seemed to be all the secrets of the cosmos.

There was something intentional, dangerously seductive, and perhaps
defiant in her smile. I can never be sure what lay behind that faint curve
of lip, but maybe it was a challenge that if I abandoned propriety and really allowed myself to look at her, there would be no question that she was
not merely beautiful—she was Beauty. I wonder if perhaps my unexpected
choice on Midsummer's Eve had slightly disturbed her confidence in the
ability to own the worship and desire of all mortal men. Maybe this was her
rejoinder to my callous claim. She seemed to say, "Just look at me—look at
me. If I have your eyes, I'll have your worship." For surely to deny a goddess
one's worship is chief among sins.

Despite all fear and all resolve, I gave in to the irresistible impulse to watch her sunrise activities from my bedroom window. Every morning was the same. Her soft, white robe fell to her ankles in the whispering grass, and she mounted her stone alter, facing the black waters with arms spread in benediction. The rising sun embraced her naked form, and there she danced, seducing the natural world into reverence through her audacious display. One morning I was sure that she had noticed me watching at my window. My face burned with shame, but I was held at the window trans-fixed by her ritual. Her practice didn't alter with notice of me, but I thought a faint smile crossed her lips as she exposed her radiant form before the sun, the lake, the birds, and me.

Mind your thoughts, Eliasz. Mind—your—thoughts.

Summer waned, and the time for my departure drew near. I stood by the lake while Erik went into the cottage for my luggage. I was left alone with Freja. Her light, billowing dress fluttered as she lifted a slender hand, placed it on my burning cheek, and turned my face to look at hers. All the breath left my lungs. All the blood left my head. In the still soundless air, I heard some alien voice rasp painfully, in tones only vaguely familiar as my own: "My God! You're beautiful!"

She smiled again, this time an exultant smile. She whispered some-thing lovely that I can't remember—just the wordless tone of her voice—then kissed my cheek lightly, turned, and left me on the gravel drive. I watched her walk away to the lake, barefoot, radiating a terrifying beauty, and laughing. It was strange, mirthless laughter that set me shivering. I gasped for the air I'd forgotten to breathe. I felt as though I had been brushed by something so terrible yet so sacred that its pure fire began to consume my mortal flesh.

On the way to the ferry terminal, Erik dominated and waxed eloquent about this perfect summer, reminding me of my responsibility to return the following year. I nodded, smiling, interjecting thanks and appreciation where it seemed appropriate, but my mind could think of little else than my previous brush with the divine. I watched his face, observing his square jaw, its powerful muscles, and imposing brow. I looked at him with renewed appreciation and respect. One faint brush of his goddess's hand, and I was nearly dead where I stood. And this was he who could meet her gaze as an equal. And she was the goddess who could inspire worship in that terrible warrior god. I was filled with awe and humility. I felt I had witnessed something not of this world, and now as I returned to the world of men, to my dingy loft with its shards of failed artistic ambition still littering the floor, I felt new inspiration bubbling in my imagination.

10

Making a Mark

IT'S NOT SO HARD to start. The pure, virgin canvas holds an irresistible attraction, whispering seductively, "come make your mark." No, there is nothing so easy as starting. All that is needed is a line. Calligraphic, contour, cross-contour, cross-hatch—flowing, elegant, decorative, rhythmical—defining, expressive, representational, implied? A line is quite simply
a point which moves—
a point which moves—
a point which moves playfully, boldly, timidly, angrily. Isn't that a beautiful thought? I take my instrument and make my mark, that moving point, chasing it across the expanse of white like a timber wolf flying across a clearing of untouched powder after a snowshoe hare. The first line is as exhilarating as it is easy.

But once that mark exists, decisions must be made, knife-edges must be walked, and the temptation to rush resisted. From that stroke onward, the chief aim is finding unity: to create variety without losing harmony, establishing dominance without sacrificing proportion, effecting motion and movement while striving for economy and clarity. Balance. Closure. Gestalt. No, starting isn't hard at all, but finishing . . .

The snow is falling on New York City tonight as I sit at my easel, warmed by memories of summer and the San Juans and by an ugly gray cardigan that wears me with confidence. It's lost so many buttons, there's just one left now, right about at my xiphoid process. Why is it that the ugly sweaters, the ones with paint splatters and pizza sauce stains, last the longest?

I'm staring at my line, quivering, shivering all alone in the snowy waste. Where am I going with you? You're lost in the cosmos, searching for boundaries—the certainty of space. You need some perspective, an atmosphere in which you can find at least the illusion of a quiet corner to hide. I'll sketch some stark contours . . .

. . . forgive me. That was cruel. I made your space equivocal. You may be cowering in your corner, but you may also be hanging projected—impaled—suspended from a sharp protrusion—dangling helplessly in the Void. The perilous existence of a moving point.

How many of these moving points does it take to distill the truth about a subject, rather than portraying mere descriptive facts? The universal invariables, as it were. I mean, I call them invariable, because the vast majority of humans are born with two ears, two eyes, and one nose—the basic framework of human anatomy. Must I paint every plane, every possibility of attitude and expression? Or can one line alone contain in its simplicity the mysteries lost in the crowd and confusion of extraneous detail and universal characteristics? I may never come closer to her truth than this one line—this point moving through equivocal space. But I can't seem to stop there. My brush guides my hand with confidence as I watch lines and shadows and curves and colors bleed over the surface of the snow. Every angle represented in one cubic form.

Fearsome, but it's all been done before.

11

Pointillism and Implied Lines

LINES CAN BE SUCH *straightforward, reliable beings. They can tell you every-thing you want to know, boldly proclaiming the simplest truths. They can also be insightful, defining what you know is there, but can't quite see. Occasion-ally, they can be devious and crooked, misleading and untrustworthy. Never completely trust a line. But learn how to read them, by all means. They are everywhere, creating texture and value, contour, and color. They can even do their best work in absentia, through implication and suggestion which the mind interprets as presence.*

I look down into the street below, where two inches of snow lie undis-turbed on the pavement. Under the orange halo of the streetlight, I observe an old gray cat walking with purpose up the sidewalk, leaving a trail of neat round tracks. I abandon my unhappy lines to shiver in the cold and prepare a new canvas. I dip the fine point of my brush in a pool of pinkish paint and begin to dot the canvas with small stationary points, like footprints in the snow. Each an eternal moment. As the traffic of thought begins to thicken, more points crowd together, close. Congregations of new colors crop up in different degrees of vibrancy and value. The prints propagate over the snow until it is thoroughly trampled underfoot, the entire canvas overspread, and every awkward, empty space filled with small, stationary points of color. They don't seem to mean much in themselves, but distance brings it all together, uncovering the Point within the points.

From across the room, all the lines suggest themselves without ever being there as her form blends itself into clarity through some optical trick. Can her truth be told purely through implication? Perhaps this is closer to the truth, after all. Perhaps the line is too confining and absolute, assuming knowledge that isn't there. But a snatch of color, the hint of a form, an emotion, an attitude, a feeling, a moment may be the clearest picture one person can hold of another, and all the details and specifics are of our own imagining. How much of intimacy and worship must be built on assumption and farsightedness? Perhaps the inner meaning of any one person's unique personhood is a divine secret, like the proverbial old man who says, "I know my wife so well, I don't know her at all." The incompatibility of the statement is both humorous and acutely real. To know someone well is to realize the degree to which they may not be known.

But these are old tricks. There is nothing new here. It's just a woman formed from many still points—a constellation of moments—as viewed from behind. If only I could get around to the front . . . the face.

12

Surrealism

FACES . . . FACES . . . faces . . . A face in the rock. A face in the cloud. A face in the tree. Everything conceals a face. I know I am on the wrong side of reality now because I can see them. Strangely familiar, deformed, ancient faces. And yet I can't see her. I thought I would find her in that awkward empty space in the middle of my picture, but she's gone. Where is my subject? Where is the dominance . . . the focal point? Is it the rock? The tree? The cloud? Those leering, many-faced ancients who have pushed themselves forward and hidden her? I make a mad search. Why isn't she in her rightful place? She belongs . . . or she is meant to fill in the empty space, right at the center of things, but she's vanished, leaving nothing but rocks and clouds and trees with primitive faces! She must be here somewhere!

I stumble backward to see what some distance can reveal. The scene, the entire bizarre picture, is a face! The lake is a grim, gaping mouth, stretching across the horizon, but my eyes are caught by something floating on the surface of that mouth. I've found her at last! She's there, clearly reflected, as though standing on the rock where she's meant to be. Her smooth, naked form is distorted by the ripples that wrinkle the water's face. The reflection floats and flutters on the surface and seems to move, but where is the solid form that casts the reflection? Is she there, or isn't she? Is it all an illusion? Is it merely a reflection of my own mind and what I think should be there? What I'm told to see? My eyes are fooling me. My mind is a muddied lake wherein float the cold corpses of oh, so many misconstructions. I'm seized with fear, throwing open the window my face is blasted by a cold that hurts . . . and darkness . . .

Perception is such a flimsy construction, so arbitrary and personal, and now I tread timidly into another man's field, for the mind is a boundless frontier inhabited by many monsters, and I am merely trespassing without a passport. There is nothing new in what I've done. How many others of my generation have "freed" their minds, explored alternative consciousness, used drink or hallucinogens (or both), while seeking to juxtapose the natural world with the dream world, looking to find some greater truth. In so doing, I abandon the imagery generated by her conscious and observable behaviors by delving into the subconscious—my subconscious—to release the tiny captive bird of truth from within this envelope of reality.

My head aches as I gulp black coffee and survey last night's work. It says more about me than her, and the face which makes the whole is so disconcertingly familiar, yet altogether strange . . . staring with bitter contempt and frightening malice . . . only when I see my reflection shimmering across the glassy surface of my coffee do I recognize that ghastly face.

I stare into my cup of coffee. I feel like I'm being sucked into its blackness. My efforts are vain. There is nothing new under the sun. Is a person a point that moves, haphazardly, circuitously, chronologically, or a constellation of many still points—many moments that converge and form a whole? They both sound right, but they can't both be. Or can they?

13

Gestalt Theory

PERHAPS STARK REALISM IS *where I should have started to begin with. Impressionistic renderings rely on some understanding of the subject's essence at that moment. For me, the moment is past, and the essence eludes me. Even realism involves abstraction, though. How can I abstract her sufficiently to reproduce her faithfully? Her eyes, her mouth, her hair, her kneecaps, and her fingertips. Yes, I have already been told what to notice. And I did—I did notice, against my better judgment. I was arrested by them, in fact, and studies of these individual elements aren't complicated. I can recall them vividly, these specific details, but when I put them all together, there's no closure. Let me make my situation clear: I've put them all in, every little faithfully reproduced feature is where it ought to be as nature decrees, but no patterned relationship occurs. They're right—I know they're right—they're true to life, or at least my memory of it. The eyes—how could I ever forget them! The lips are certainly accurate, the nose beyond perfect. The whole shape of the figure appears true as well, but a unified whole simply isn't emerging.*

I know how it's supposed to work. When the required elements are grouped correctly, final recognition is achieved unconsciously by the mind of the one looking at the representation. What have I forgotten? The parts are all there—I've checked—she's not missing an eyebrow or a nostril. Everything is in its proper place, but the complete form refuses to materialize.

Is it me? Is it her? Or is it my image of her? It's true, my skills in perception have been called into question recently, but I see the dalmatian in the dappled light under the tree. I see both the young woman in the big hat and the old woman with the big nose. I'm good at those optical illusions. My mind is functioning, healthy, undamaged—maybe even quicker than most at perceiving images through emergence, reification, multistability, invariance, and prägnanz. I get gestalt. I'm good at gestalt. I remember the class—I was awake for it—it rained that day, and the professor was late. I understand what's supposed to happen and how to make it happen. The problem must be the parts—a false grouping of incongruous parts. For this, I can only blame faulty memory, for noticing the wrong things or for at least recording them wrongly. That must be the problem.

But she is hard to look at—hard to really see. And yet she's impossible not to notice, like Erik said, in her particular details . . . the eyes, the hair, the backs of her knees. Still, a whole picture of Freja is so hard to discern, either from shyness about looking too long or too hard, or the distraction of those alarming perfections that force themselves to be noticed.

I'm quite obviously not ready to paint her yet. Not until I can see the whole, instead of the separate, perfect parts. And I am tired. I am so very, very tired of snow and gray, of cold and cars, and being alone, except for that face reflected back at me from the old metal teapot. It would have me believe that not only is my cup as big as my head but that there are actually deep furrows between my eyebrows, and I'm most certainly not frowning. A lemon wedge the breadth of my shoulders . . . it's all to be expected since they sit closer to the pot, and I am sitting back from it. But those furrows—trenches, you could call them—they do disturb me. How angry I look! And I'm making no expression at all. My face at rest looks angry . . . why?

How difficult to distinguish between
what is and what merely seems.

14

Spring Out of Season

I'VE BEEN TOO MUCH alone. I know I have. All winter, I've been too much alone, shut up in my loft. I've drawn her—I've painted her. I feel I've found something. Something is starting to come clear, though I need to see her again. But I feel weak—frail even. I need to be out, to move and breathe, perhaps see other people or at least be in the same place as them. I'm trying today. There is a little hole-in-the-wall restaurant owned by a family from India that I've passed coming from the station and smelled the warm spices. I've finally come to sit. She brought me masala chai. It looks all cream and steam and smells like every good spice in the world has found its way into my cup. It tastes good, too. This is between mealtimes when no one is here to eat. Only a few people have come to have this cup of otherworldly goodness, and now she's brought me some sort of sweet as well.

I have the best seat, by the window, to watch life going on outside. An old lady is sitting at the other window by herself. She was here when I arrived and will probably be here still when I'm ready to leave. I've seen her before walking in my neighborhood. She looks like someone's grandma. I wish mine were here. She could sit in the empty seat across from me. We would smile across at each other and look out the window at the trees. They are just beginning to bloom. We would marvel to each other: Can it be spring already? Isn't it too early? Did it happen this early last year? I hope the trees aren't thwarted by some sudden cold snap. Isn't it such a shame when things happen out of season? The frozen blossoms of the apple tree fall like snow on snow—just a heap of futurelessness, now wilting and brown edged—life that could have been. Fruit never to form, or ripen, or nourish, or even return to the earth

60

containing new possibilities. There's nothing sadder than what might have been. The life cut short . . . the childhood interrupted.

I'd talk to my babushka about the past—the olden days—the way things were for her. I'd learn about her mother, her father, her grandparents, all the things she remembered. I know what to ask her now. I'd listen to her stories, some repeated and some new, but I'd listen to them as if they were all told and heard for the first time. We'd sip our chai and nibble our sweets and maybe even get a refill. No, no, my treat, dear sweet Babushka! My treat! And then I'd ask her who I'm like. You have your father's jaw and your mother's eyes. You have great uncle Pawel's nose—he had only one hand, you know. Only one hand. I don't remember how he lost his hand, but he was an artist, like you—a beautiful, beautiful artist with his one hand. He died before you were born. A part of me would leap inside with the discovery that I'm like the ones before me, that they loved art and trees and mosses and birds. Perhaps they would have loved the pigeons and my other gutter friends.

I'd hand her my sketch pad, and she would leaf through it, gasping over the trees and birds and table fruit. It occurs to me that she wouldn't like the studies of Freja. You've forgotten her clothes, Eliasz! That poor, cold woman will catch her death! Then looking at me through narrowed, crinkly eyes, she taps my head with her primordial talon.

Mind your thoughts, you naughty boy!

But Babushka, it's not like that. It's not like that at all. All artists will study nudes.

A different word for the same thing, you naughty boy. You use words like that woman's makeup—to cover the truth underneath.

There's no winning the argument, and so it falls away. Even now, I feel her disapproval, though she was never here at all. She is of another, more prudish, old-world generation. She doesn't understand my work. Poor thing, it is beyond her. We'd change the subject, retreat back into the mist of the past, the people who came before, to Uncle Pawel with only one hand, and all the rest.

I'd find out who I am and where I'm from. She'd help me navigate these questions. She would tell me you are very new. You are very new and very old. You are at your beginning, but carrying within you your end, which you try to reason out by what has come before. But maybe it's the same. Maybe your end began the day I held you in my arms—the day your mother delivered you into this world. Perhaps birth only happens once, but death is every moment.

We need our grandmothers to teach us the art of dying well. Mine disap-peared too soon—before anything made sense—before the stories, the lessons could leave their indelible mark. She had promised to write to me, those years ago, and I had promised I would sit down every day and draw her pictures of all that I saw in my new home. And yet within a year, I stopped finding her letters in the box, and my drawings went on arriving for someone who was no longer there. A cancer in her body swept her fast away, and we didn't even know until some months later. She had died in the springtime, and that's how I think of her still. Like an early spring blossom touched by the frost. Death out of season. Like my father and my mother, both. The futurelessness of snow on snow.

So, I just sit here, pretending I'm not all alone. Pretending that death isn't now and that every moment is a beginning, not an end. Every moment is forever, and the apple blossoms will always ripen into nourishing fruit. All seasons know their timing. But the cup is almost empty, and the spices are bitter and gritty at the bottom. It's time to go. I'm just loitering now, loitering in a life that seems like someone else's. But I will care for myself, Babushka. I will. Yes, I promise. I will take care of my health. I will eat my brown bread and stop smoking like Dedushka, and yes, of course, I will draw a big, warm coat for my lady on the rock.

PART II—1975

1

Unsettling Returns

I can't remember who told me this, or maybe I read it somewhere, that the original joy of experiencing a new place can never be repeated—that experiencing someplace new is like a loss of innocence, leaving childhood behind in a cloud of nostalgic dust on life's meandering tracks and backroads. Going back is futile, like revisiting a childhood home. Memory records the secret hiding places, the creaks of stairs, the damp smell of forbidden crawl spaces, the garden rows and insect faces, the personalities of trees. The grownup person returns to find something small and alien where nothing is quite as remembered. Dull disappointment mingles uncomfortably with the insane perception that the place is haunted.

I suppose plenty of people encase their happy childhoods and those familiar spaces in a shrine of sorts. Even unhappy childhoods, or those brought prematurely to a screeching halt by loss, can be mentally smelted, refined, and recast in a happier form. It's probably a mercy that we can't manipulate time and space to return to these "happy" days. We might realize that they were a fantasy of our own creation, or something painstakingly orchestrated by loving parents who made humbler things shine with significance and value when all the world was going mad around us.

Maybe it's better to give in to that long, subtle process of lying to one's self over decades and revising memories until an ideal replaces reality. Idealized nostalgic trips are as serviceable a way as any to distract the mind from wandering too close to the approaching darkness. And so it is with travel. Look, that certain someone told me, always and only for new experiences and never try to revisit past places. Once you've left it behind, that place will never exist for you again except as a beautiful memory. Chasing after it again only taints the original experience.

When I found myself watching rural America fly by me again on the Greyhound bound for the extreme occident of the country that next summer of 1975, it felt like nothing could be farther from the truth. It was not only as beautiful as I had remembered, this diverse slice of the land of the free in all its purple mountain majesty, but more green, more bright, more sparkling and surreal than when I had left it, the seed of inspiration just taking root in my brain. It was like returning to childhood from the practical and colorless world of adults, and realizing that I was indeed a child again, not just an adult visitor. I once again possessed those young and thirsty eyes that see everything as sacred.

Basking in my own inner world, I only comprehended snatches of conversation on the bus and enjoyed it as background music—the soundtrack of my journey. I relished the timbre of high and low voices, the suprasegmental pitch changes and tonic accents, the shapes of vowels, the textures of consonants, the colors and flavors of words that held no meaning or importance to me at that moment, beyond the aesthetic.

The previous year's darkness and depression had hindered my ability to really see, hear, and enjoy life, or to realize that life was even happening. The gloom of that time had made every day seem like a small, stagnant eternity, waiting for life to start while failing to realize that it already had, and was running ahead without me. Now I felt the thrill of motivation and the surge of life—that it was happening now and that I needn't wait for it any longer because it wouldn't wait for me.

I had been sick that previous year from lack of inspiration. I was weak from neglect of my body and the physical activity needed to save me from actually wasting away into the blackness I perceived creeping ever closer. But after returning from my first summer in Washington, I felt inspired not only to paint but to make an effort to care for myself. Erik's fastidious upkeep of his physique had caused something beyond the usual sense of admiration with a pang of jealousy. It led me instead to look at myself critically and with dissatisfaction. Upon returning to New York after that first summer, I sensed mounting intrinsic motivation. After a year of slow but consistent exercise and mental activity, I felt confident that I was a stronger, better man than I had been the year before. I was still just an ordinary mortal, but one who could carry his own suitcase. Now I stood on the upper deck of a Washington State Ferry once again, the wind whipping in my hair, returning to my original mountaintop for more vivifying midsummer inspiration.

As my ferry approached the familiar terminal, and I finally stepped into the small crowd of meeters and greeters ashore, I scanned the milling populous for Erik's face. I didn't see him, so I sat on a vacant bench near the water to wait. Ferries came and went and, with them, their companies of sunbaked passengers. I compared my watch to the clock at the terminal. Erik was late.

I was anxious to be on my way to the cottage and especially to the lakeshore with my sketch pad. After some innocent people-watching, I sketched some quick studies of faces waiting to board the next ferry. They all seemed to be so happy like there was nothing they would rather be doing than waiting for that boat to arrive, which would take them to who knows which island or back to Anacortes. Perhaps I projected my own happiness at being back in the San Juans onto those faces I sketched, all of which seemed to beam with innocence and *joie de vivre*. A wrinkled old couple, the man with his arm resting lovingly on the woman's shoulders (how I love drawing wrinkles), a young family with two blonde-haired twin boys who must have been about three years old, bursting with energy and constantly moving. They ran up and down the platform racing and yelling to each other in their own personal dialect. I knew what they were saying, though. Boys are boys, and I was one myself once.

I indulged in the study of a middle-aged man's singularly shaped nose. He talked on a payphone with the kind of smile that convinced me there must have been a pretty woman on the other end. There were a few people lying on their backs in the grass with sleeves and trouser legs rolled up, letting the warm rays ripen their skin like summer fruit. I observed a bald eagle picking flattened days-old rabbit roadkill off the pavement, most indecorously. Two hours passed as I sketched the faces and forms at the ferry terminal— sketched the indecorous national raptor. Boats arrived and departed. New faces replaced old ones. I began to worry that Erik had forgotten me. I didn't have his number to call, and my mind began to run through the few options I had for finding assistance if he didn't show up soon.

At length, I saw him. That same robust figure striding towards me with a confident and unapologetic grin. He looked disheveled as if he had recently woken up, his face overshadowed with several days' worth of stubbly growth. His bloodshot eyes fixed on mine as he boomed a greeting.

"So, you're here at last!" He clapped me in a rough, minty embrace.

"At last? I've been here for over two hours."

"What? You came on an earlier ferry? You should have told me!"

"No, but I told you before I left—"

"You must have told me the wrong time. Never mind—are you hungry? I have some smoked kokanee back home with your name on it. Caught and smoked it myself! Just wait till you see my new smokehouse! Freja thinks it stinks, but the magic it works on a fish! You'll see—you'll see. Let's go."

Erik reached out to grab my largest suitcase. As the muscles in his arm rippled and bulged, I felt that old jealousy resurfacing, until I noticed a slight tremor in his hand. I hadn't remembered that from before but soon forgot it as we loaded my things into his car and sped off to the cottage down winding roads flanked by thick forest. That hadn't changed.

I entered the stuffy, stale-smelling cottage to find dishes, socks, books, fishing lures, and broken shells resting in odd places, and most of the shutters closed. Erik laughed and shrugged his massive shoulders. He offered something like an apology, explaining that he'd been living the bachelor life for the past month while Freja was in Los Angeles visiting her mother, seeing the sights, and "the typical LA stuff." An older woman from town came to clean and stock his pantry once a week, and she was due sometime in the near future, but he couldn't remember when, in fact, he thought he might have told her not to bother since he kept such odd hours lately. Or had there been a grandchild born? He couldn't recall, but it didn't seem to concern him. Erik assured me that my room was clean and ready for me to create world-improving art in it. He sent me upstairs with my things.

When I joined Erik on the deck later, he had a plate heaped with whole smoked kokanee, heads half-way attached, and shrunken eyes glaring up at me. Next to them sat a bucket filled with ice and beer. It felt almost as if I had never left—no preliminaries, pleasantries, polite chitchat, or updates—just a slight pause in a conversation that rambled along as naturally as a shorebird picking through pebbles and shells for its breakfast.

"Don't you ever think of finding someone?" Erik asked with his usual blunt authority.

"What, to clean my loft? Afraid I can't afford that kind of luxury, but at least it doesn't take too long to clean 300 square feet," I joked.

"What? No! Come on! You know what I mean: Someone!"

"You mean someone to go to bed with every night and wake up with every morning, who knows all my faults and weaknesses but loves me in spite of them? Someone who will drink coffee with me every morning in that silence, which is never awkward, but which only comes from knowing someone so completely and so comfortably that words are superfluous . . . someone to hold my hand when I'm old and flabby and take me to play bingo? You mean someone like you have in your perfect goddess, Freja?" Erik took a long slow suck at his cigarette then exhaled with equal languor.

"Something like that. Maybe not the bingo—I'd rather scoop out my own eyes with a melon baller! I'm serious. But someone you can adore above all others, who can fill that hole in the heart of every man. Someone who can make everything make sense in all this madness and give you something to believe in. A true guiding Polaris. A Someone."

"It sounds wonderful, but what would someone like that be doing with me?" He laughed. "No, but honestly, that's a great deal to expect from any one person, don't you think? I mean, you got lucky. It's harder than you'd think to find someone perfect enough to be worshipped—loved, maybe. But even that's more complicated than it should be. At this point, I doubt I'll ever find her again."

"Again? Oh, I get it—unrequited love. Happens to everyone at some point, I guess. Not to me, obviously, but I hear tell. A popular trope in most genres, I suppose because it's so immediately accessible to so many. Well, my friend, that defeatist attitude isn't going to help you find her! You're a good person Elias, and I mean that. One of the genuinely good ones—not a fake—but you're shy, that's your problem. You need to put yourself out there more, or don't you want to be happy?"

"It's not that I don't want to be happy. I mean, who doesn't? But I'm not getting any younger and if I haven't found her yet . . . I don't know, assuming she even exists, maybe she's gotten tired of waiting for me and found someone else by now. That kind of someone can't be short of followers, and what's so special about me that's worth waiting for?"

"Ugh! You depress me! You really do! You are so incredibly passive! I just don't understand how you live at all. No thought of your future—your lineage—your legacy. I mean, what about children?" he probed.

"Children?"

"Sure! You never pictured your life with two or three miniatures tearing through it—pass on your genes, your wisdom—that nose of yours?"

"I suppose every painting is, in a way, my child. It's certainly a labor of love bringing them into the world," I mused.

"Well, that's very maternal of you," Erik said with mock gentility. "No, a true man wants a son—someone to teach things—to tell things.

You know, the important things. A boy he can take out into the woods, chop things down, catch things, carve things, shoot things. A man wants to know that he's leaving something of himself behind in this world—a legacy or something—an heir. Or at least someone who will remember him and share his name." He trailed off as he lifted his glass to his lips, staring out over the lake and sighing a thin stream of grey smoke through pensive lips. "That's what a real man wants."

"You and Freja thinking about starting a family, then?" I asked. My question pulled Erik from his reverie, and he rose irritably from his chair.

"All in good time, you know. We're awfully swamped at present. I'm in the process of writing an epic poem about the end of all things from the perspective of the sun. It's going to shatter everything they've come to expect. Language that no one has used before. Gloriously profane. Tells it like it is. It's going to be my greatest gift to humanity yet. But eventually, a man of greatness needs an heir, you see, to carry on that line of great men back to Harald Wartooth, you know, my ancestor. He was a king, you know. I've told you about him, haven't I?"

"I remember."

"A Viking king. Legendary. His father was Hrœrekr Ringslinger, you know, they say he was Prince Hamlet's grandfather. Can you imagine! Well, anyway . . . it may not be time just yet for my son and heir to enter the scene, but I can picture him: a serious-minded little blond-haired boy. I can teach him how to catch and gut fish, how to behave with honor towards a woman. I can take him on rambles through the woods, you know, shoot pellet guns at robins on sunny summer days. You were a boy once . . . can't you picture it? A boy I can share all my wisdom and knowledge with. Well, the time will come." He reached for his beaver tail. "But, until then! Grab a paddle—let's chase the sunset."

A mauve mist faded upward into the deepening twilight as the warm orange glow from the windows of the cottage became mere pinpricks on the distant shore. As the lights disappeared from view, I worried that we might not be able to find our way back again in the dark, albeit brief, night. I remember feeling cold and watching the darkness gradually swallow up rocks and trees, obscuring the boundary between lake and land, reality and imagination. My mind filled the blank of darkness with all sorts of fears and horrors, and I remember raising an invisible hand at one point to ward off the maddening nothings that swarmed closer and closer around me. But Erik kept plunging his paddle into the still black water, rhythmically, tirelessly, as though every stroke brought him nearer to some personal and tangible goal, invisible to me in the obscurity of night and ignorance. I wanted to say something, to break the silence and ask what it all meant. I didn't dare speak, and the only sounds were those of water lapping against the ribs of the canoe, and Erik's paddle plunging into the black depths. He showed no sign of stopping.

2

Consequences

Papa would often tell his boy the ancient tale of how the birds chose their king. The birds decided that he who could fly the highest would be named the true king of the birds. Everyone thought that the eagle would win, with his majestic wings stretching tall as a man! However, as the eagle spent his strength rising higher and higher, he grew arrogant and thought that he had won. He lifted his sharp, hooked beak to the sky in triumph and started coming down to claim his crown. But there, hidden under his tail feathers, flew the tiniest bird in the forest, and as the eagle came down, the little bird kept rising. That is why the firecrest wears a crown. Because tiny though he is, he is the rightful king of all birds.

The little boy lived out the story in his dreams all night. The little bird was him. He was the tiny firecrest who would be king of all birds—not the eagle. He flapped and soared on the air currents—rising—rising—rising—ever upward and into the golden sun.

It was still dark when Papa put his hand gently on the boy's sleeping head. The boy, still riding the warm air currents on tiny wings, blinked a moment, then suddenly jolted upright. He rushed to pull a frayed gray sweater over his tussled head when he realized that it was time. Papa was taking him deep into the primeval forest before sunrise to see a real family of firecrests.

The chilly air filled the boy's nostrils and lungs with the wholesome smell of damp soil and trees just waking from a long winter's sleep. He held tightly to Papa's strong hand and skipped by his side. The little boy's stomach fluttered with the excitement of seeing the king of the birds from the old story, but also with the exciting prospect time alone with his papa before anyone else was awake.

When they reached the perfect spot, the two of them sat motionless and silent on a damp stump. It was so early that even the birds were still sleeping. They kept as silent as two mushrooms on that stump, as though they had grown there overnight. The damp seeped through the little boy's trousers until they were fully saturated and cold. He felt like getting up and dancing around to warm his stiff, chilly legs, but didn't give in to the urge. He wanted to show Papa what a good bird watcher he could be—how still and quiet and patient. And he had to be patient for quite some time.

Finally, just when the little boy thought he couldn't wait a moment longer, Papa tapped his shoulder and pointed silently into a giant ash tree. There amid the sprinkling of sticky new leaves, was a tiny dark body stirring. Its head flamed with an orange crest. There was its crown! Peering around, it finally greeted the morning with a peal of twittering song that echoed through the forest. The startling music sent waves of ecstasy tingling from the top of the little boy's head to his cold toes.

That one individual's call

was answered by another—

—followed by another—

—and another—

—until the trees all around them were alive with the firecrests' song. Papa watched the boy's enraptured face as he looked from tree to tree, trying to spot each singer.

Papa answered all his questions as they walked home, never interrupting, and always trying to find the best words to reach the heart of the little boy's curiosity. When he didn't know an answer, he promised he would try to find out, and somehow, he always did. From the nature of that strange powder found on moths' wings to the reason for the variety in beak shapes between different species of birds—the boy's curiosity was caught up in the magic of ordinary things. Papa was patient, never sarcastic, ironic, or cruel. He reserved any judgments and criticisms, only ever radiating love for the boy skipping by his side and dreaming of flight.

"Do you know everything, Papa?" It seemed to the little boy that his father was a fountain of wisdom and knowledge that never went dry.

"Oh, Eliasz, your papa knows so very little."

"You know more than me. I think you must be the wisest person in the world."

"I may know a few more things because I've lived longer, but wisdom isn't about what you know in your head—like the names of trees or why their leaves change color in the fall."

"What is wisdom, then?"

"Oh, my sweet boy . . ." he paused to find the right words for a precocious six-year-old. " . . . the greatest wisdom is humility. Humility is wisdom of the deepest kind. It's knowing who you're meant to be and that you're not that person yet. It's seeing your own failings instead of everyone else's. Sometimes it takes us grown-up people a lifetime to realize how little we really know, and how small we really are. Some of us never learn. Others believe they have wisdom and humility and take pride in it. But it's only a delusion, you know, a big joke that everyone can see but him. Like a man assuring onlookers that he has a special way with animals while a pack of hungry wolves tears him to pieces. I hope you and I can both come to know the wisdom of humility in this life. It will be our salvation."

"How do you know if you're humble or not, Papa?"

"You don't. It's not something that you are, or you aren't. Humility is an endless road on which it's impossible—and unnecessary—to judge your own progress. You just keep going. Humility is an endless road, Eliasz. Endless and perilous."

"Well, I think you're very humble, Papa." Papa laughed his wholesome and wonderful laugh. A laugh without malice or mockery in its cadence.

"I know you say that in love and innocence, but it's something you must never say to a man while he lives. Nothing can cause him to stumble more quickly on that road of humility than being told he's succeeding. Best to speak of such things when they can no longer harm him. Now, should we race to the gate?" They ran, and even though Papa's legs were so much longer than his, Eliasz reached the garden gate first, as usual.

Papa was the best, most humble man Eliasz would ever know.

Dawn broke in the early hours just as we were returning to the shore. The air echoed with the nostalgic sounds of birds waking up. I slept soundly until noon when I helped myself to a simple breakfast on the deck. Erik eventually joined me, bearing strong coffee.

"Oh, Erik! I've meant to ask you . . . what about those photos from the garden party last year?" I spoke while crunching a piece of buttered toast in an effort to seem nonchalant.

"What about them?"

"I mean, what do you think of them . . . how'd they turn out?" He looked at me suspiciously through the steam rising off his coffee.

"Why do you ask?"

"Well, it's just that I had some interesting conversation with, you know . . ."

"That girl? I thought you might be going there," Erik murmured through an exaggerated sigh.

"I know. The whole thing was awkward. My fault, and I'm sorry. But I've been curious. We talked quite a bit about art. I'm just wondering what her pictures are like." Erik was hesitant, almost cagy, looking at me out of the corner of his eye.

"Well, I guess there's no harm in satisfying your artistic curiosity. After all, it's just us menfolk here. Let's get our coffee onboard first, though."

"Okay . . ."

"Always, Elias—always, always coffee first."

I'd never been in Erik's room before. I was a little surprised that he even had one. He explained that he and Freja kept such different schedules that they would only disturb each other, thus the separate rooms. The room had been initially his study and was furnished with a massive mahogany desk, shelves of poetry, one shelf devoted to several author's copies of his own published volume, a small bed, and a nightstand. Midsummer photos overspread the walls, from the first summer he and Freja spent together up to the present. Every year he had commissioned them for his own enjoyment, these icons of his wife in their garden during midsummer. The fashions changed with each year's installment, but the motifs—white daisies, natural light, soft grass, and Freja's unchanging youth and freshness—were always present. The walls of his room were a shrine to her beauty and midsummer. Sliding open a desk drawer, he produced a large brown envelope, scattering its contents on his desk.

"I mean, just look at them! They're a mess! They're all wrong! Let me tell you, it takes a miserable lack of talent to take a bad picture of Freja. She's perfect from any angle. But that stupid girl went and did it somehow! I particularly specified Ektachrome! That's what those National Geographic photographers are using for cheetahs in the jungle, and it's brilliant. The age of monochrome photography is well and truly past! As if all that gray wasn't bad enough, I don't know what she did, but Freja looks . . . she looks old! And scared, and small, and . . . just old! Gads, I can't even look at them, they're just . . . wrong!" He shoved them at me in disgust.

I studied the pictures myself slowly, carefully. There was something disquieting about them. I can't, even now, in retrospect, deconstruct the images to the point where I can explain them to my satisfaction, but I know how they made me feel, and it was chilling. They made me feel a shadow of apprehension, as though something catastrophic, some terrible disaster, was looming unseen but sensed through some other faculty. Maybe it was partly the black and white with its countless shades of gray that drained the life and blood from the scene, shrouding everything in a stifling gloom. I feared that I was seeing either a gross distortion of the truth, or actually seeing the truth for the first time—a heavy truth I couldn't have guessed, and couldn't quite put into words.

There was some implied emotion, disturbing, apart from the subject, or maybe radiating from it. What was it about those pictures? Was it a trick of the light that made Freja's face in one appear blank and featureless, like a real and physical glimpse into the Void itself? Maybe it was a mistake in the aperture. I don't know precisely what aperture is or what can go wrong with it, but I've heard the word used by those who know. Erik said Freja looked old, but it wasn't in the reality of her features. Freja's soft, smoothness of complexion made her seem child-like, but her exaggerated shape and the clothes that made it focal suggested a sexual maturity and self-conscious allure. It was an incompatibility, I believe, that created something like the visual rhetoric of a distressing joke. Was it irony?

In essence, the apparition in the photographs was a paradox—a woman-child whose eyes, though creaseless, staring out from the taut porcelain perfection of her face, gave the uncanny impression of advanced age and experience, like a prostitute wearing a child's clothes. It all felt entirely and horribly wrong. The body and skin were those of a young woman in her 20's. It was only the eyes, some ineffable quality about them, captured here in a way that had remained hidden in person (or had I never really looked in them out of fear?) that made one begin second-guessing that assessment.

Surrounded by the pure simplicity of the wildflowers, one had the distinct impression through juxtaposition that Freja herself was being exposed through contrast as a flower of a different sort. The photographs had magnified the impression of something cultivated, pruned, and shaped. How had she achieved this? Freja looked tragic, like something begging to be looked at. Not a wildflower blooming in secret for a day only to wither by evening. Hers was a studied, scientific beauty which was never caught off guard, but always poised and ready for admiration. It wasn't that the woman in the photographs wasn't beautiful. It was a distressing, unnatural beauty, stripped of the golden midsummer magic that created the illusion of freshness and youth. It was a beauty that felt wrong.

In one of the pictures, Freja seemed so small, fragile, and vulnerable, trying to be seen to advantage, but on the brink of annihilation by the forces of nature itself. Was it her beauty itself that was the illusion or had the photographer used some illusory trick of forced perspective that made the subject appear so small and frail, dwarfed by ancient, sinister trees and cruel, cutting blades of grass? This wasn't the scene I remembered observing a year ago. What twisted experiment could taint a scene so simple and lovely with such fathomless tragedy? My emotions vacillated between disgust and fascination.

"Yeah . . . well, they're certainly not what I expected."

"They're wrong!" Erik boomed. "They're just wrong! You see it too?"

"There *is* something . . . I don't know . . . can I keep them in my room for a while, spend some quality time with them and try to figure it out?"

"Keep them! Burn them! Do what you like with them! I never want to see them again!"

"Well, they're certainly something else. I'll ask her about them—try to understand, you know, what she was going for."

"That little girl playing with a camera? You won't be seeing her here."

"She's not coming this year?" I don't know why I was surprised. Hadn't she told me, after all?

"Not a chance! She's gone, Elias." You won't see her here on the island. I doubt you'll see her anywhere within a thousand miles. The pictures would've been enough on their own to earn a painful exile in Seattle, but you! Well, you know what you did! She could be in Greenland and not get a job taking pictures of icebergs!"

"Me? You don't mean that stupid contest?"

"You didn't think there wouldn't be any fallout, did you? Someone had to pay up. Better her than you, I say. You were just naïve, but she was . . . vicious!" I stared at him speechless. "What's wrong with you? You look like someone left your baked goods in the rain!"

"I didn't know . . . how could I have known?"

"Just be glad that it wasn't you who suffered excommunication. You've received the grace of a pardon. Take it . . . and the lesson."

"But it's not fair! Those pictures were obviously a fluke! She's still learning. The rest was my fault, not hers. I'd rather take the heat now than live the rest of my life knowing I ruined hers!"

"Don't be an ass! You don't know what "heat" is! Do you think you'd be here now, painting those world-improving pictures of yours, if Freja hadn't judged in your favor?"

"World-improving! Whose world?"

"Look, it was bound to happen one way or another. When you consort with a goddess, sooner or later a sacrifice is required. All things considered, you got off easy. Someone had to pay, that's all there is to it. Balance is restored now. Just be glad it wasn't you."

"But . . . isn't it enough not to hire her again? Why all this drama?"

"Don't be simple." He gripped my shoulder hard. "Just accept it and move on. Now stop moping! Unless guilt helps you paint, it's a useless emotion."

I left that afternoon to sit alone at the coffee shop—the one where I had found her the summer before and talked like a pretentious ass. I sat there for two hours, drinking more coffee than is healthy, examining the photographs she'd left behind. She never came. Of course, she never came. I don't know why I had half-expected that she would. In my mind, I had held out some hope that she was just having one of her strange jokes with me when she said goodbye. That she would show up, flashing that inscrutable grin, to help me decipher her work. I stopped by her mentor's studio. When I asked how I could contact her, he only shrank from me as though I were a dangerous madman and asked me to leave. I began to understand. She had become one of perhaps many who had paid a tithe to Freja. Not only had I made the mistake of praising her publicly (an offense which I should have paid for), but she had dared to imply an alternative narrative with her pictures—a narrative I was barely equipped to guess. My mind was troubled and confused—angry and yet terrified. I returned to the cottage, determined to behave as though nothing was amiss, though I began to suspect that more was wrong than a few midsummer photos.

3

Remodeling

THERE'S MORE THAN ONE way to fill a hole. I hesitate to say this absolutely—I'm no longer young enough to know anything with much confidence—but I think one of the most common ways to fill the Void is with work. This aggregate of survival, success, self-sufficiency, ambition, exceptionalism, and obligation adheres nicely, covering over the cracks that naturally form in the decorative barriers we construct to block the Void from immediate view. These cracks may only be glimpsed from the very corner of the mental eye when one is quietly resting, causing rest itself to become a fearful state.

Is this why the businessman avoids his accrued vacation? And when he takes it, keeps busy repairing the house or taking trips chasing new experiences and constant motion? Is this why he spends his evenings watching television or ball games or drinking at the bar with loud friends? Is it the fear that when everything stops, when he is still, quiet, and alone, that aggregate of business and busy-ness will crumble, revealing some appalling truth he's been trying not to notice? Even the trust fund supported man of leisure who is not obligated to work for survival can make himself busy with projects and ambitions enough to cover the cracks.

As that second summer progressed, I found Erik changed. Not essentially, no one changes essentially without chemical imbalance or near-death experience. No, he was still himself only restless. He couldn't sit and look out at the water for long, blowing smoke rings, and enjoying the quiet as he had seemed to the summer before. He moved with agitation from one task to another, without ever finishing one. He busied himself with extravagant and highly detailed plans for his midsummer garden party. He busied himself with refinishing his wood-strip canoe and rubbing out the scratches accrued from beach pebbles and subaquatic branches. He busied himself with alphabetizing the books on the shelves, the spices in the cupboard, the files in his cabinets. He even began to clean, scouring sinks and chipping mineral scale off the faucets, constantly talking to himself as he worked. His small-scale mania seemed to peak in his ambitions to publish yet another epic poem, this one a futuristic hero's tale of conquest over the mighty forces of nature on the inhospitable planet of Mars. He expected it would be a crowning achievement, another gift to posterity, yet he never seemed able to sit down and write it. How could he focus on art, he would ask, when there was dust on the ceiling fan blades?

His cleaning, however, was frantic and distracted as his mind took random turns, and he would become unnaturally animated about every little curiosity that came to him. One such curiosity burst from him one morning while I was decorating an English muffin with some ruby colored jam.

"Gymnopaedia!" he shouted, causing me to drop my muffin, which fell, as they always seem to, jam side down on the floor.

"What?"

"Gymnopaedia! What is it?"

"I don't know . . . songs for the piano?"

"No, but what does it mean? The word."

"Are you *really* asking me, or do you already know what it means, and you just want to tell me?"

"No, no . . . what an arrogant fellow you must think me, Elias! I don't know! I think it might mean walking around naked . . . or maybe barefooted? I've been told the former before, but do you know, I think an argument could be made for the latter!"

"Well, I—"

"I must know! I must find out! How can I find out?"

"You do have multiple dictionaries, Erik. I saw you shelve them in your "D" section yesterday. Why don't you just look it up?"

"Look it up in the dictionary? What kind of man do you think I am? No! No, I've got to reason it out! I've got to find the answer myself."

"What if *I* were to look it up?"

"Treachery! Don't tell me! You'll spoil it!"

"I could just let you know if you're getting close . . . "

"Would you do that?"

"If you like."

"And you'll tell me if I'm hot or cold? If I'm way off, you'll give me hints?"

"Sure, yes, I can do that for you."

"Not big hints mind you. Just little ones."

"Little hints, naturally."

"Do it! Do it! Do it now! Get Oxford—I don't trust Webster."

While Erik was initially disappointed that the word didn't mean bare feet as was his pet theory, he seemed satisfied with his proximity to the historical meaning. He seemed even a little interested in the ancient Spartans and their naked dancing youth. However, within a few seconds of satisfying that curiosity, he had moved on to a different curiosity, and I finally got to decorate another muffin. Such was his mania, that I laughed at him and even with him, yet wondered to myself why he was acting so oddly.

One morning that summer, my body still rigidly bound in fitful sleep, I had a disturbing dream. I was on an old steam train, moving swiftly through the sunny summer countryside, when a massive, rolling earthquake rippled over the landscape, derailing the train, which crashed with such force that the boiler exploded. My limp body was pulled from the wreckage and, although I was merely unconscious and badly broken by the impact and projectile debris, the people who discovered me thought I was dead. Worse than that, they thought I was someone else. I was shoved into a cheap coffin, just some rough pine box, given a brief and unremarkable few words of eulogy in which they referred to me as the old house painter from the town yonder, owing to the paint on my trousers, and planted me in a grave marked Damian D'arco: May the Selfish Bastard Rot in Hell. When I finally regained consciousness, I was terrified by the darkness and the cramped space. I pounded and pounded, shrieking for help—for mercy. "I'm a good person!" I yelled. "You've made a mistake! I'm alive, and I'm not selfish!" I pounded my fists, splintered and bloodied, on the rough coffin lid, but no one came to my rescue or to Damian's, for that matter. The name, in the end, didn't matter. Neither of us was worth saving. And yet I kept on pounding,

pounding,

pounding . . .

When I jerked awake, sweating and relieved, I came down the stairs to a cool breeze flowing unchecked from a jagged, toothy mouth ripped open in one of the perimeter walls of the cottage. Erik stood, sledgehammer in one hand, bourbon in the other, with a wild grin on his unshaven face.

"So that's what all that pounding was. Some wakeup call!" I said, trying to sound casual.

"Just doing a bit of remodeling. You know, I've always wanted a room just for my books! As it is now, I've got books in my study, books in the guest room, books in the living room, books in boxes packed away . . . hell, I've got books in the kitchen cupboards! I don't know why the devil I haven't gone and built myself one before. I see it as a dark wood-paneled room with floor-to-ceiling bookshelves and one of those rolling ladders, and a bust of Aristotle! He was clever, that one. Maybe even a fireplace, or a wood stove or something! That Persian rug I've got rolled up in the closet, some nice warm lamp lighting, a leather armchair . . . with wings! And I've got this statue! I've always wanted a place to display it properly. Freja can't stand it. Doesn't like the competition, I expect. You really should see it."

"Not the bronze goddess with all the arms you have in your study closet . . . the one wearing your bathrobe and hunting hat?"

"That's the one! Lakshmi. Brought her back from India in the bachelor days."

"I don't think that's Lakshmi. It looks more like Kali to me."

"Whatever. It's all the same. Oh! Now here's an idea! I could have one of those antique-looking globes that's actually a bar! You know what I'm talking about. You slide back the top half, and there are Scotch and crystal tumblers inside. I can smoke my pipe in the winged armchair and crack open a rift in Siberia whenever I want a seismic snifter! I can count on your assistance, of course? Wall hangings, floor coverings, furnishings, textures, color schemes, the artist's sense of proportion, and so forth?"

"I'll help if I can. Am I permitted a cup of coffee and some toast before I'm put to work?"

"Of course—hierarchy of needs—get yourself in a creative frame. Go, go, help yourself! I'll get out the graphing paper and pipe tobacco."

Ripping open his home to the elements seemed to me like a massive dislocation of his senses, baring not only his physical living space to the light and air but exposing his private mental chambers to public view. In this shucking off of the usual, the ordinary, he had stripped away the last veils of pretense obscuring his deep discontent. I did as he asked. I sat at his desk with a piece of graphing paper, my pencil frantically flying as he paced the room, flinging contradictory dictates as to both the contours and minute details of his ideal space.

In one moment, the sketch had all the decorative self-indulgence of the Rococo, every space filled with ornamentation of some sort, intricate cornices and ceiling panels, gilded façades. In the next moment, stark modernism, all straight lines, and primary colors took over. Another moment, it had to be rustic with paneled walls hung with badger taxidermies and knick-knacks made of bullet casings. The space had to be cozy and low, expansive and buoyant, dark and contemplative, light and airy, soft and hard, quiet and musical, rustic and refined—an impossible space. Amid all the mental switchbacks and indecision, the one action finally taken was to bandage the mangled wall with sheet plastic until we were ready to build.

That time, however, never came. When Freja finally returned from LA, looking even more youthful and beautiful than I had remembered, her first action was to contract builders to repair the wall. Erik didn't object audibly, though he might have muttered "treachery" under his reeking breath, and peevishly retired to his workshop to re-refinish his canoe. He would take me aside periodically after that, quietly trying to persuade me of his case that a creative genius needs his own space to follow his whims and fancies, and how a real man must work with his hands and make things himself.

"We're *homo sapiens* . . . we're *homo faber*! We men are creatures that must both think and make! Think and make! Think and make! Think and drink and make love and drink and think, and . . . and make, and . . . oh, treachery! I really wanted that book room!"

4

Freja's Studio

AFTER FREJA'S RETURN AND Erik's remodeling debacle, I spent more time on my own, either hiking with my sketchpad or painting in my room. An awkwardness had settled on our interactions, as though I'd received an unintended leak in confidential intelligence. I felt both of their embarrassment about what had transpired. I felt embarrassed myself for seeing something I wasn't supposed to see, and so I kept to myself, only occasionally visiting other rooms of the house where I might meet one of them. My most frequented space, beyond my own room, was the kitchen, to which I was left free-reign, and which neither of them visited often.

I frequently woke early, finding sleep difficult in those early hours with sunlight streaming into my room through the curtain lace. I would quietly rise and walk down to an alcove with a window seat, partially concealed by heavy drapes which, if drawn shut, created a private reading nook. There I would sip my morning coffee, jot pretentious observations in my journal, and look out at the lake in silence. Erik and Freja rarely stirred before noon, granting me relative certainty against any awkward encounters. The window seat was within view of the door to Freja's room, but I rarely saw or heard anything from within, and by the time she was up and moving, I was out with my easel on some distant trail. Certainly, I was avoiding more than awkwardness. Truth be told, I was even more scared of her than I was before since Erik's revelation about the fate of my photographer friend.

Sitting there each morning lingering over my coffee, I had often imagined what Freja's room must be like. It was the private space from which she emerged and to which she retreated, always alone. My wandering mind imagined almost religious mystery at the heart of that space and flowing from the goddess who lived in it. In my mind, I pictured it as her inner sanctum, a room pregnant with secrets, and I could only guess what supernatural radiance blazed behind that always closed door. In my early morning musings, I pictured it as the bedchamber of an ancient queen, all gilt statuary and marble columns and palm fans—perhaps some rose petals scattered picturesquely across the shining marble floor—the heavy scent of incense and perfumes filling the air. That cinematic scene was still projected in my mind when the silence was broken one morning by an unexpected creak from that very door. Startled, I turned from the window to see Freja's grey eyes fixing me in an unwavering, unapologetic gaze. I compulsively looked away, looked down, looked out the window, and burned my mouth on my coffee. Perceiving her gaze still fixed on me, I finally, nervously, met eyes with her. Silently, and in all solemnity, she summoned me.

Freja and I had never spoken much, beyond terse pleasantries and those words of obligatory welcome and farewell that pass between hostess and guest. My place was made clear from the beginning as Erik's pet, and one whose existence she would merely tolerate. Had she been ugly or even ordinary, I would have been offended by the suggestion of such arrogance, even considering my own social ineptitude. However, since I was still dazzled by her, believing her to be some divine archetypal Beauty, I considered myself lucky just to look at her. This morning was no exception. Her face was all radiance, and her hair was pure sunlight as her firm and shapely arm beckoned to me in a confidential gesture which, up to that point, had been utterly unprecedented. Erik wouldn't stir for some time yet. Filled with wonder, I quietly obeyed, passing the threshold into her inner sanctum.

"Come sit with me, Elias. You're so aloof lately, and I'd like your help with something." She chided me, almost as though we shared a history of verbal discourse, even of friendship, in which I had rudely lapsed. I found myself mumbling apologies as she gestured toward a modest armchair where I was meant to sit as though I'd done it a thousand times before. She sat across from me on the edge of a small but neatly made bed, watching my face with quiet condescension as I glanced around timidly, trying not to appear too curious. There was no grand, sweeping canopy, no palm fans, no freshly scattered rose petals. There were no candles or alters or incense. I had not walked into the holy of holies, but rather into another artist's studio.

Freja's room was full of mirrors in varying sizes, angles, and magnification. A well-lit vanity displayed the artist's palette of moisturizers, creams, foundations, powders, pigments, pastes, brushes, sponges, swabs, pencils, crayons, individual and whole sets of lashes, lacquers, paints, hot irons for curling, hot irons for straightening, switches, extensions, sprays, gels, bleaches, brushes, picks, and countless other devices I couldn't hope to name. On the floor by a full-length mirror was a set of dumbbells ranging in weight from five to fifteen pounds, and other physical fitness devices for pulling, pushing, lifting, squatting, crunching, and curling. What I saw in Freja's room was far more secret than any of the divine contingencies I could have imagined.

"Erik talks with you about us, doesn't he?" she began abruptly, pulling my attention away from her studio supplies and back to her canvas.

"Sure, I mean, not a lot lately."

"But he confides in you."

"I suppose so."

"He tells you the things he wants. The things he thinks will make him happy—things he thinks are his right to have?"

"I'm not sure I—"

"Come on, Elias, don't be coy. I'm sure by now Erik has told you he wants a son."

"Oh, that. He did mention."

"I knew he would. He can't think of much else right now. Everything always comes back to that. At first, I thought it was a passing obsession, but it just doesn't seem to pass. He tries to distract himself, but the way he does it! It's getting more extreme . . . more exhibitionist. That book room! He's just embarrassing himself now." I nodded quietly. What could I say? Of course it was true, though I wouldn't have had the heart to say it aloud. "You must . . . no. No, I don't mean that. Will you—please—use your influence? Will you talk to him . . . as a man?"

"Oh, wow. You know, I don't think I should interfere. It's really not my place to even have an opinion. Haven't you talked to him?"

"Of course I have, but he can't understand . . . he could never understand why it's impossible. If he did understand . . . well, he just shouldn't. He doesn't need to."

"I'm sorry, I can't. . . this is none of my business. Your . . . these things should really be between you and Erik."

"Don't be a prude, Elias! It's probably not even what you're thinking. In fact, I'm sure it's not. This is nothing new, you know. That's the real tragedy, is how predictable it all is. You men are all the same—and always the same.

You have a beautiful woman before you, you enjoy her and maybe even worship her for a while, but it's never enough. You're a man, so just like the rest, you can't understand! You worship a woman's youth and beauty, and you think having a child won't change anything! You fixate on it like it's the only thing in the world that can complete you. It's just so predictable. Well, it can't happen."

"Look, I don't want to make assumptions, but I'm sure . . . in fact, I'm practically positive that Erik's love for you is stronger than this obsession with having a son."

"Love? What does love have to do with it? If the goddess of Beauty loses her beauty, loses her youth, and the fertility that makes it all the more seductive and dangerous, is she still a goddess? What do you think I would become to him if he stopped seeing me as perfect? Stopped seeing the possibility and the danger? Don't you understand? I would lose him! To lose just a piece of that whole is to lose it all. He just has to decide, or believe he's decided, that he doesn't want a child after all—that he's content with things just the way they are."

"But how do you bring him to that when he's in such a place?" I asked. She looked at me searchingly.

"All I'm asking is that you try to convince him. Reassure him. Remind him of my beauty and boost his ego by praising it yourself! It's okay, Elias. It doesn't even matter if you don't think I'm the most beautiful woman in the world, but make him believe you envy him. Tell him that it would ruin my beauty if I had a child."

"Would it, though? Would it really? I don't see why it should even matter since he loves you so very much."

"You're still talking about love. It's my beauty he worships—I can't lose it!"

"But I don't know what I would even say to him. This is crazy . . . "

"You're a painter—paint him a mental image of some silly old cow with dimpled thighs, thick ankles and stretched, sagging udder—ridiculous and absurd, begging for him to kiss her scars out of some sense of gratitude! Make it grotesque! Make him afraid to lose me as I am. You tell him—in your own words—don't tell him we've talked. Be subtle. He needs to think these thoughts are his own."

"Well . . . I mean, I guess I can try . . . "

"That's all I'm asking. You're a good person—humble and good—he'll listen to you. He trusts you."

"Well, thank you. I will try, but I just have to say . . . I've heard some men say they think they're wives are more beautiful to them with age and motherhood than they ever were before. Lots of men say it, and I know they mean it."

"You don't understand. Some things just can't be . . . they aren't for you or for anyone else to know. Anyway, I couldn't bear the condescension."

"Why condescension?"

"Can you really believe that a when worship is gone, contempt doesn't take its place?"

"Why should contempt take its place? Why not love? Surely love is just a more temperate, more forgiving form of the same thing." She looked at me with an expression of pity which I hadn't expected.

"You haven't known love yet, have you? Poor Elias. You haven't known it at all if you think it's more temperate. It's not—it's just different. Love, when lost, ends with mere indifference, but disappointed worship can only end in the deepest hatred."

"But why should that be? I've never seen evidence of anything that dramatic."

"You don't believe me because you haven't seen it yet, but trust me, if you just live long enough, you will."

"And you've lived long enough to know all this from experience?" I said incredulously.

"Well, I didn't have to experience it, did I? I knew someone who did. It's wise, isn't it, to learn from the experiences of others? It can spare you a lot of suffering by observing theirs."

"True enough, but I've never seen this, even in someone else's life."

"Well, I knew a woman a long time ago who was celebrated for her beauty. She married a handsome young man who worshipped her, and they were gloriously happy—for a while. Not many months after they got married, though, she was pregnant. She was glad because she thought that a baby would only make them happier. But as her body changed, his attitude toward her changed too. After the baby was born, her body was covered in scars. Her face was tired and puffy, and you know it wasn't long at all before he left her forever, I suppose for a younger, more beautiful woman."

"So, you're saying that she loved him, but he worshipped her, or rather he worshipped the way she was . . . the way she looked when they first married? But how could there be no love left? You said they were gloriously happy?"

"She did love him, I think. If she hadn't, she might not have loved their child so much. But there couldn't be any love left in him, simply because there never was any, to begin with. Don't you see? Worship is powerful—love is also powerful—powerful and consuming, but they are a different species. Sometimes you can't tell the difference when you're young and in the throes of emotion."

"Well, what happened to them? Your friend and her child?"

"What else? He left her with the impossible task, in those days, of raising her child alone—no family to lean on—nothing. They survived, but just. Now I'll ask you: how could that child escape growing up believing that there is no person in the world more hideous to the eyes than the person you can no longer worship? That child not only inherited her mother's beauty, but she learned her mother's lesson, as well: that worship is fragile, difficult to maintain, and above all temporary. That being the case, when you find yourself at the center of another person's universe, you should never, *ever* get too comfortable, or trick yourself into believing you're loved. Only a man who truly loved his wife in all her fragile imperfection could look at her when she was an eighty-year-old great-grandmother and still see a beautiful young woman."

"You mean . . . you don't believe Erik loves you?"

"He worships me. It won't last forever, of course, I know it can't. It never does. But surely it doesn't need to end quite so soon, and so messy. Does it? Won't you please consider talking to him? Talk him down from this mad dream of 'posterity' and an 'heir to his fortune and name.' Just talk to him. Please."

"I will. I promise."

5

Choices

SHE HAD SCARED ME, of course, since the moment I first saw her, if only because of her terrible beauty and resemblance to an undying spirit. My fear intensified with the realization that she could, with a word, a nod, a whisper in the right ear, pronounce sentence on whomever she chose. She had punished my sin against her beauty in proper goddess fashion by requiring a human sacrifice, and yet, after our encounter in her room that morning, my perception of Freja began to shift. How much of her beauty was clever artistry and the confidence to play a part? If, after all, Freja had some "imperfection," she was careful that it should never be seen or guessed. Where there is imperfection, there can be no true worship. Of that much, she was acutely aware.

While it is perfection that we worship and ideal beauty to which we build our shrine, it is imperfection that we love. It is vulnerability that we cherish and feel the urge to protect. It is human frailty toward which we feel warmth and a tenderness of heart: the weak, weary bird that rests in our hands and tells us its woes, trusting that we won't cast it away to be trampled, but kiss its feathers and hold it close. It is the dimpled cheek, the constellations of freckles, the crooked smile, that wisp of hair that refuses to stay put, the broken heart that seeks a confidante, the shy, the timid, the injured, and beauty unaware of itself. I could bow before the perfect beauty that Freja claimed, but I couldn't love it. Here Freja's words rang true to me. It wasn't about love. It never had been.

It wasn't about love, but with me, it could now no longer be about worship either. By inviting me into her studio, into her concerns, her insecurity, her pain, and her past, she had acknowledged humanity and, therefore, imperfection. She had sacrificed my worship on the chance that I might be able to help her maintain Erik's. But I still couldn't believe her theory about worship turning to contempt. I had convinced myself that when my worship of her perfections died, my pity was born. I felt pity for the woman who saw her person and her place as so wholly dependent on a youthful body that she couldn't bear a child, fearing above all imperfection and losing the ability to inspire worship. Yes, I believed I pitied her quite sincerely.

I couldn't judge her, I thought. It wasn't, after all, my business whether she and Erik were honest with each other or not. But here I was the chosen mouthpiece, the representative she had elected to plead her case. Was that quite fair? Was it right that an outsider should have an opinion, let alone state it? But no, that wasn't a concern since she had freed me of that responsibility. All she asked was that Erik hear her opinion from my mouth and be led to her conclusions while believing them to be his own. If only it had occurred to me then that I could have said no.

Maybe it's dangerous, looking back on the past and identifying those few choices that should have been more carefully considered. For me, it has been those moments when I have said "yes." I have rarely regretted a negative, few though I've given. But for a young man of my insecurities, "no" was a difficult word to articulate. For someone prone to hero worship, there is no more wonderful thought than that one's heroes should return the compliment, or at least place a little trust. It was refreshing and exciting because they seemed to need me rather than just put up with me. In saying "yes," I was not only Erik's confidante but Freja's too. In those immature times, I felt more pride than apprehension.

That night I dreamt that I saw Erik and Freja, standing on the edge of a steep cliff. They stood well apart, as though some invisible force repelled them from each other, and gazed individually down into the canyon below. I started to walk toward them. I walked with such blazing confidence! Where did that confidence come from? I didn't mouse-trot like a cowering mortal man at the feet of a great god and goddess. I was the god, and they were the mortals. They looked up at me with sadness. I kept walking toward them. I walked past them. I didn't slow down. I walked with unflagging confidence straight off the edge of the cliff. I walked off the cliff, somehow knowing it wouldn't be me who would fall. I walked off and immediately began to fly. They watched me in amazement and admiration as I soared aloft on the wind currents like an eagle. They tried to follow me, but when they stepped off the cliff, they plummeted to their deaths.

I woke with a jerk. That was not an acceptable ending. I lay with my eyes pinched shut, trying to replay the dream with a more appropriate conclusion. In this revised half-waking version, I swooped down impressively and caught them both, one under each arm, just inches from the jaws of death. I returned them to safety. Their gratitude was beautiful to behold— the tears of joy—I believe Erik might have kissed my hand. Freja kissed my cheek. I was extraordinary, and I had saved them. I would save them now.

Humility is an endless road, Eliasz.

6

Hatching a Plan

Everything was different in New York City, just as he had suspected it would be. The tall, glistening buildings, the cars—so very many cars—the noise, and the way people acted with each other. He didn't like it. He missed sleeping on the floor by the stove, holding onto Babushka's old orange cat, who purred in his ear until he drifted into warm and pleasant dreams. He missed Dedushka's snoring and found it difficult to sleep without the assurance of the old man's comforting presence nearby. He didn't feel safe. He missed the music of night insects and the wholesome smell of soil and clean animals. Yes, everything was different in New York City.

The little boy's mother had quickly found employment cleaning office spaces, and she worked long hours. It was summer, and little Eliasz had nothing to do—no one to be with him until Mama returned to their little room in the evenings. It was hot. He opened the window to invite in a breeze that smelled of sewer gas and old cooking grease. He lay on the bed listening to the horns of cars down below. He lay so still that anyone would think he was sleeping. Sometimes he was. Mostly he was waiting.

When Mama returned, bringing a can of tomato soup and a small loaf of bread, the two of them ate together, slowly, without speaking. She was too tired to speak, and he knew it, but she held his hand. They prayed before a small icon of the Theotokos tenderly holding the little Christ child, then turned out the light to sleep. But he couldn't sleep. He had to keep watch. He had to keep at least one eye open to monitor that dark, shimmering shadow in the corner. If he looked away, it came closer. If he fell asleep, he feared it would descend and consume them, because one night, it almost did.

That night he had fallen asleep on his watch when suddenly he sensed the dark shadow bearing down on them as they lay sleeping. He jolted up, screaming and flinging his arms and legs wildly before him as if to fight off the unfriendly specter. Mama jerked awake, quickly turned on the light, and tried to calm him down.

"Hush, Eliasz. You'll wake the whole building, and they'll make us leave! Hush, there's nothing there! It was a bad dream, only a bad dream. Dreams are only pretend; they're in your head like a story, but they aren't true. Everything will be okay. There's nothing to fear. Breathe deep, my love."

She wrapped her arms tightly around the little boy. His whole body felt awash in a wave of terror so profound that he feared it would drown him. His heart pounded in his chest, temples, and ears. What was this creature who could dematerialize so quickly in the light? Mama could never see it, but he knew the truth. It never left. It may be in his head, but that didn't make it less real. He would have to be extra vigilant at his post from now on, for Mama's sake. She was tired, and quickly drifted back to sleep, still holding onto Eliasz. He lay as still as possible to avoid disturbing her, all the while keeping watch on the shadow in the corner, keeping it at bay.

As an adult, it is easy to sentimentalize childhood, packaging it up neatly in the warm, colorful wrappings of innocence and joy and wonder and nature. I remember being a child. I also remember being afraid. I think all children are afraid, beset with all the complex inner conflicts and suffering that we've convinced ourselves were absent in that brighter age. One could create a catalog of childish fears, but perhaps nothing frightens children more than that moment at bedtime when the light goes out. The room swarms with things unseen yet imagined so vividly that they become real. Friendly elements turn hostile, and toys come to life. The child screams, and Mother runs in. The menacing creatures of darkness fade in her presence as she sings softly, stroking the child's hair and saying there's no need to fear. But that, as we grown-ups know, is a well-intentioned lie. The world is replete with adults who fear the darkness more in old age than they ever did in childhood. I am one.

What do children actually see in the dark? We tell them it's their imaginations and nothing more in hopes that they will stop letting themselves see these things at all and go to sleep. But how do we explain our own fear of that darkness—that teeming emptiness that we try to ignore? Or do we, like our child-selves, allow some bigger, stronger person to tell us everything will be okay or allow some pharmaceutical aid to numb our anxieties and coax us back to sleep? It may be in our heads, but that doesn't make it less real.

If my friendship with Erik up to that summer in 1975 could be depicted as one line, it would be a vertical one. I had always been the cup and Erik the jug. He was the repository of wisdom and knowledge, and I was its willing and eager receptacle. He was good at giving advice, and I was good at thinking that I needed it. Freja's task, therefore, required a change in the angle of our friendship. I was a cup caught between two jugs, the one asking me to fill the other with some of its own contents. I was caught in a farcical situation—a child sent to cajole the parent into seeing the specter of impending oblivion as nothing but a bad dream.

That seemed to me to be the real issue. Erik had felt his mortality. He had felt the approaching darkness that we try so hard to believe isn't there, and he was afraid. He was afraid of oblivion, of leaving behind nothing of himself, no trace of his existence to be celebrated or at least remembered fondly. He aimed too high with his poems, hoping to create some epic legacy for himself. He saw his chance for ultimate salvation from utter annihilation in producing an heir—a child—a piece of himself that would survive and perhaps leave behind another piece. He was looking for immortality, and it was my job to talk him out of it.

I mulled over my words, laying on my bed in the long dusk, staring at the ceiling. I thought I wanted Erik to be happy. I was convinced I wanted them *both* to be happy because I was a good person and a good friend. Perhaps it was in my power to reignite their happiness. I applauded my own altruism, for what could I possibly gain from helping ease their marital tension? By reinforcing Freja's status as Erik's goddess divine, I gained only the satisfaction of seeing my best friend happy, and perhaps finally gaining Freja's approval of my existence—even her gratitude. The thought of rising in both their estimation made me rise in my own. I decided this worthy endeavor of re-mystification would benefit everyone.

As I continued to muse on the virtues of my involvement, and my own selflessness and goodness, the desire to help grew to missional proportions, and washed over me like a wave, the power of which I could not resist as it carried me away toward what rocks, reefs (or rewards) I couldn't guess. Was that really what I felt? Was I so naïve? Could I genuinely have applauded what I had tricked myself into seeing as purity of motive and selflessness? I blush now at this foolishness, though I won't wholly rob myself of good intentions toward my friends, knowing at least how earnestly I believed it at the time, but I now know the near impossibility of a truly unselfish act.

The Self can only be kept from the center of one's universe by mammoth acts of asceticism and self-denial, and even so, in the quiet solitude of a desert cave, in the hunger of fasting, in the exhaustion of vigil, the Self struggles to escape, to run unchecked toward its basest desires. Perhaps even the moment of martyrdom is stained with doubt, recoiling from the nauseous stench of self-sacrifice. And I did see my involvement in those terms—as a saintly outpouring—giving aid to my friends.

The surface of things looked pure enough, but much of the force behind my desire to help was the secret, subtle, subconscious desire to be admired myself. I had long been the one admiring my friends, and this new shift in the terrain of our relationship had upset the previous balance, putting me in the position now to be admired for my salvific efforts on their behalf. I say it was subconscious because, though it was there, I would not allow myself to acknowledge it. For what is the subconscious but the mental storage unit for all the desires, memories, feelings, and experiences we don't want to be aware of? And I did not want to be aware of those chronically sick and feeble insecurities—the tendency to see myself as a black hole in the company of stars, grasping greedily at the chance to feel soothed and made bright by some little reciprocal admiration.

Motivation, that nebulous fog of subconscious reasoning that drives the simplest of acts can often only be recognized in retrospect if at all. And in the dread moment of decision and implementation, we allow ourselves to believe the most ghastly lies about ourselves. And I did believe. I believed in my mission to help, I believed in its rightness. I believed in my own goodness, never for a moment considering that I was only helping myself as I set the scene in my mind, prepared my words, and waited for morning.

7

The Tale

HUMANS ARE FANCIFUL CREATURES. We love a good narrative, and if that narrative is received through some highly believable, immersive medium, so much the better. Part of it is escape—defecting for a while from reality, its pain, its fears, its darkness. Life is full of well-scripted dramas both on the stage and in private life. Pretense suggests a life full of certainty, and every wordsmithed morsel of wisdom we dish out is to convince ourselves as much as those around us that we are okay—that they are okay—that everything is and always will be okay. We act our part as best we can, choose our words, our reinforcing non-verbals. I think the Bard said it best. He knew our condition—mere players acting out strange parts on a global stage.

I set my scene on the lake. The canoe, having finally dried after its re-refinishing, was again seaworthy, and Erik and I were overdue for a fishing trip. It was a perfect morning, and Erik needed an occupation that he couldn't abandon after five minutes. I chose the boat for that purpose. He could change seats, he could feel as though he was moving, but he would still be in a boat on a lake and couldn't escape me.

We hooked our bait, cast our lines, and he opened his flask. In the brief quiet of that moment, before he could grow agitated from the stillness, I chose to begin my soliloquy:

"I've been thinking about what you said when I first arrived, about how I need a special someone in my life. I mean, you're right, I'm sure, but I don't know how I can ever be happy in this life if there is only one Freja in the world, and she's yours." This tempting hook got his attention. He wiped his now smirking lips and began to expand visibly.

"Well, there are lots more fish in the lake, Elias. Not quite so fancy as mine, of course, but . . . "

"That's the problem. You really are a lucky man, Erik. I will never have what you have. I can only believe that one perfectly beautiful goddess exists in the world, and she's yours."

"She is that! Mine indeed. My goddess!" He continued to swell in his seat as I fed his ego. I pushed on with mounting confidence.

"Anyway, if I were in the position of being the luckiest man in the world, on the very brink of greatness in my poetical career, respected, admired, envied . . . married to the most beautiful woman in the world, I would probably just find a new reason to be unhappy. It's my nature, you see, I'm restless. That's just me; I can't seem to make contentment stick. It's not my nature and never has been. I know that if I were to fall into the magical situation you're in, I'd get bored and start wanting this or that or children or something, and then, you know, my perfect goddess's perfect body would get all mangled from that ordeal, which, you know, I've heard stories . . . and then where would I be? I'd have gone and spoiled what I already had and be even less contented than before. Up at all hours with screaming babies, changing diapers, too tired to create anything worthwhile, let alone anything great, and my muse would turn matronly and lose interest in me in favor of our plump, pink progeny."

I was feeling pleased with my performance, complete with carefully planned alliteration, even though it didn't in the least express my own feelings on the matter. Still, I'd at least delivered it with panache and had remembered some of the more arresting non-verbals I'd so deliberately prepared. His response, however, was slow in coming. He didn't look at me, but watched the surface of the water, rippling with little water insects, before finally speaking.

"I never took you to be a materialist, Elias. I thought you were made of finer sensibilities—a spiritual being, in fact. That's it—a spiritual being who occasionally indulged in the odd physical experience. I'm disappointed." Erik said, shaking his head and finally looking at me, his eyes filled with pity. "No, I'm more than disappointed; I'm shocked that you, of all people, would marry a woman just for her beauty! After all those sensitive observations you made about morning coffee and comfortable silence and bingo. No . . . wait a second . . . " He paused, his eyes narrowed, examining my face. "No, you're not talking about yourself at all right now, are you. You think I married Freja for her beauty. You're talking about me, aren't you?"

"Well, didn't you? That's all you ever praise about her—her perfect breasts, her hair, her eyes, her fingertips, the backs of her knees—what am I supposed to think?"

"Well, it's true, she's the most beautiful woman in the world. Women want to hear that. They need to hear it, both outright and whispered behind their backs by men who can never have them. If they don't, they get insecure."

"Freja's not insecure, though, is she?"

"She knows how I feel. She thinks I wouldn't see her that way anymore if she had a child."

"Well, would you? Or would your object of worship become an object of contempt?"

"Now you sound like Freja! I adore her! She's my goddess and if she lost her figure giving me a son—" he paused, taking a generous gulp from his flask, "—she'd just make more trips to LA to 'visit Mother.'"

"What does that have to do with anything?" He looked at me out of the corner of his eye, waiting for the euphemism to dawn on me. "Wait, are you saying . . . "

"There it is! You're surprised?"

"Well . . . how much?"

"Who knows. I don't ask."

"You don't mind?"

"She's beautiful, isn't she?"

"But it's not . . . "

"Natural? You show me a work of art that didn't have an artist."

We sat in awkward silence. My scene hadn't played out as I'd imagined. I'd lost my train of thought and wasn't prepared to improvise my way out of the situation.

"You're right, though, Elias." Erik finally said. "I've chosen a different kind of someone—a different kind of experience than you ever would. You can't have it both ways. No, you're right. Even if I never reach my potential as a poet or have a son to carry on my family name and remember me when I'm gone, if I can't find contentment being married to the most beautiful woman in the world, I could never be truly happy. Of course you're right. You're a good friend, Elias—a good person. You make a lot of sense. It is silliness, all of it. You're right. Of course you're right."

8

The Appearance of Success

DURING THE FINAL WEEKS of my stay, it seemed that the bitterness and discontent which had prevailed like some kind of brain fever in Erik were finally breaking, and a new ideal was growing in its place. He was inspired by a renewed intellectual asceticism, which seemed to elevate his mood and reclaim a degree of serenity and sense of well-being through submitting to a more austere rule of life. This new life included total abstinence from liquor before 5 pm and whole days spent in silent stillness and abstract thought or tending a garden he had started on one side of the house. He even had a burst of creativity, resulting in some new poems. He wasn't entirely satisfied with them but seemed at least hopeful that continuing his new regimen would lead to better outcomes in his writing. I thought the tide was finally turning, and that my powers of persuasion had prevailed. His new healthier lifestyle encouraged me that he was on the path to physical and mental recovery. I believe I knew even then that it couldn't last. Perhaps it would have ended anyway, but the rabbits didn't help matters.

It was an unusually hot afternoon, and I had been examining my sketches from the morning in an armchair by the window when Erik stormed into the house. He had been weeding his garden, which generally made him irritable anyway, but this time his anger was so explosive that he could barely speak. His red face was streaked with sweat and flecked with soil. His hands were shaking in tight fists.

"What's wrong?" I asked. "What happened?"

"Rabbits!" he finally said in a low, murderous tone.

"Rabbits? In your garden?"

"Yes, yes, of course, in my garden! Where else would they be—the powder-room?"

"Well, did they do a lot of damage?"

"What do you think?"

"Well, based on your face—"

"Everything! They dug under the fence and ate everything, the treacherous little savages!" Erik waved his hands overhead as if to include the sky and clouds in his definition of everything.

"Oh, come on. Not everything." Erik looked like he might strangle me. "Why those rascally rabbits. Did you see them?"

"Did I see them? I saw the whole damn warren! They must've called over the country cousins to join in the feast!"

"So, they ran away?"

"Ran? Ha! They galumphed!"

"They . . . ?"

"Galumphed! No, I've known the word of old, I've just never seen it in practice until today. They galloped—triumphantly! They galumphed—they pranced—they shook their damn tails at me, they sneered and jeered and the ring leader—some scrappy buck with one ear up and one hanging down all wopsical over one eye—he looked back at me and screeched some rabbity insult over his shoulder. I don't know what it meant, but I do know it was a challenge!" Even in his rants, Erik paid close attention to word choice, and I tried not to smile.

"What will you do now?" I asked.

"Do? I'm getting my shotgun and waiting behind the blackberry brambles till they come back!"

"What? You're not going to hurt them! What good would that do?" His eyes were bulging from his face now.

"Satisfaction!" Erik roared. "Vengeance! Defending my property against the marauding hoards! The thrill of nailing that wopsical bugger in his wopsical head!"

"But they don't know the difference between your garden and everything else. They're just hungry!" I said, pleased to hear the echo of my father's voice in my own.

"Yes, well, I'm hungry too! Hungry for *hasenpfeffer*!" Erik stormed back out and viciously kicked a tree trunk several times in a row, knocking loose some strips of bark. When he finally stopped, he came back in to rant a little more.

"If it's not the damn rabbits, it's the damn deer. All the damn natural world wants my cabbages!" I perceived he was actually enjoying his rage—the strength of the emotion—the novelty of having someone to participate in the scene with him—so I played along.

"Oh! I've seen some of your deer every morning! They're magnificent! There's a doe with twin fauns who comes around almost every morning for a snack!" I let a big innocent-looking smile spread across my face.

"You mean you've been spectating while the vermin make a snack out of my garden every morning, and you haven't done anything about it? You haven't even tried to scare them off or anything?"

"Erik, come on. They don't want your garden. They come for the snacks I leave for them. Bread crusts, apple cores—stuff like that. What crumbs they leave behind, the blue jays clean up a little later."

"Crabs and crumpets, Elias! Now let me get this straight! You've been inviting these pests onto my property, giving them free food from my pantry, and just watching them trespass? Oh, treachery! Treachery at every turn!" Erik was incredulous, or at least he thought he was.

"I like them," I said simply, shrugging my shoulders. "Not something I usually see at home in the city."

"Oh, what next? Soon you'll be telling me you've given them names . . . oh no, spare me! You have, haven't you?"

"The doe is Imogene. Her fauns are Speckles and Spook. Spook won't let me feed him by hand yet," I said ruefully.

"Oh, better and better—you're a deer tamer!" By now, he was smiling and only pretending to be angry.

"They're not tame. No, definitely not tame. They're just used to me. We converse . . . commune, if you like."

"And tell me, oh wise one, what do the deer tell you?"

"They say your garden is lovely, and they wouldn't dream of damaging your cabbages, you know, unless times were desperate." He was laughing now—I'd won.

"Okay, okay! Just please tell me you haven't made peace treaties with the rabbits—my sworn enemies."

"The rabbits. Well, I've tried to befriend them, but their distrust runs deep," I explained. At this point, my work was finished. Erik was laughing. His anger, though violent while it lasted, could be defused through humor—a trick I'd learned as his roommate.

"Fine, fine. I make peace with the natural world on one condition."

"Name it," I said.

"You'll help me build an impregnable greenhouse!"

"Done!"

And we did. We wasted no time in erecting a greenhouse where his old, violated garden had previously grown. It was a greenhouse to protect the tender shoots of something new—a new life and new ambition—to coax them along without fear of wind or hungry animals coming and ravaging them. We did build that greenhouse, and, for a while, it was a very good thing indeed.

> How very like a tender, lonely child. Are they all the same? To gather a strange family around himself for company, comfort— to give and receive some little kindness in a world that seemed cold and hostile. The little boy had lain stagnant in that cramped room—lain sad and anxious—waiting until he could wait no longer. Finally, when he felt he couldn't bear the loneliness of his life in New York City another second, he came down the front steps and opened the door on its creaking hinges. Cautiously, he sat on the front stoop in the shade of a small, sickly tree and waited for something to happen. It was there that he met his first friends— the feathered family he would love so fiercely.
>
> It was only one at first. The deep rolling coo, and the scratching noise of claws peeking out the ends of clumsy pink toes, the first sounds to signal its presence as it sat lazily in the rain gutter above his head. The boy and the pigeon regarded each other casually as if to say, 'I see you.' They looked at each other long and hard, the pigeon's head tilting from side to side, as though it was thinking—trying to decide the future of this encounter. A thought came to the little boy's mind. He slipped back into the room upstairs, slid his hand underneath the pillow, and found a dry hunk of bread he had been saving for his midday meal. He took a piece of it back down the steps. Holding it in his hands while looking up at the pigeon, he rolled it slowly between both hands to form crumbs. He placed half of the crumbs in a little heap on one side of the step, then sat still on the other side. He was a patient boy. He waited.
>
> How long did he wait? As long as he had to until the pigeon fluttered down to inspect his token of friendship. The gesture found pleasing, the bird gobbled the mound of crumbs completely, then looked again at the boy on the step. Slowly, the boy opened his hand, showing the bird the rest of his crumbs. How long did

he wait? As long as he had to until the pigeon waddled over and timidly picked the crumbs from his open hand.

A friend to one bird will soon become a friend to many birds. As the boy repeated this ritual daily, not only his first friend joined him on the stoop, but gradually more of its kind every day came to share in the boy's crumbs until more and more of his meager lunch went to the birds. They sat on his lap, shoulders, and head. They preened his soft hair with their beaks. If birds can show love to people in any genuine way, they showed it by coming to him and sitting with him whether he had crumbs to share or not. Whether they truly loved him or not, the lonely little boy loved them and was no longer a lonely little boy, but a friend of many. Being with them made him remember his papa and the firecrests and made him feel like all of that wasn't gone forever. He was still himself, and he was his papa's boy.

Who was it who first said all good things must come to an end? And why must that be so? For the little boy on the stoop, loved by the pigeons of his tenement, it seemed he had finally found happiness and felt it would stay forever. But one day, as he loved his birds and they loved him, a band of bigger boys, free from school for the summer, saw him and his friends. They couldn't just look and laugh, then let him be. They looked, laughed, yelled, charged, and frightened his flock of friends into frenzied flight. Horrified and furious, the little boy shook his fists, yelling at them in the only language that would come to him.

"Why would you scare my friends like that? They weren't doing you any harm! Go away! Go away! Leave us alone!"

"Listen to the stupid Polak!" they jeered. "What's he saying? Sounds like he's saying, 'I'm a little sissy boy who plays with birdies and only knows sissy Polak words!'"

"Go away! Go away! Leave us alone!" he said again, trying to push them away from his stoop.

"Get him! Let's teach the sissy boy a lesson!"

When the bigger boys had finished with Eliasz, he lay in a crumpled heap on the sidewalk. Blood flowed from his broken nose, and the bruises on his punished ribcage from the kicks they'd given him would take some weeks to stop hurting. He lay there, not crying, not waiting—for who would come to him? There was no one. He lay there thinking about the boys and their cruelty. He thought of their size and their strength. The frightened birds slowly, cautiously, flew down and gathered around their injured friend. He just lay there ruminating over his many wordless thoughts while his nose made a little dark pool on the pavement.

How can it be? How is it possible to hate something and admire it? To hate it and envy it? He thought about how big and strong and fierce the other boys were. He hated them for what they had done to him and his friends. He hated them and wanted to be just like them—to have such power and strength and influence—to become everything that intimidated him about them, but to use it differently.

9

Silence and the Octopus

ERIK WAS SATISFIED FOR a while with his new greenhouse, tending its inhabitants with obsessive care. However, without the drama of animal invasions, gardening eventually became just another silent activity, and it wasn't long before that silence, which seemed at first to restore him, became a deathly vacancy—an empty and loveless hell teeming with fears and obsessions. He finally seemed to lose all focus and motivation. Abandoning the distracting hobbies and ambitions that had at least kept him moving, his frenzy slowed to a dazed halt. He sat staring out the window, seemingly paralyzed, either lost in swirling thought or at a loss for even one.

This was an Erik I hadn't seen before, and it concerned me. I would leave him staring outside from his armchair while I was hiking and sketching, sometimes for hours at a time, only to find him exactly as I'd left him when I returned. There were whole afternoons I would sit with him in silence waiting for him to break it. Finally, somehow or other, I would have to.

"Have you ever thought of keeping bees?" My voice sounded absurd to me after the long quiet, and the question I'd chosen even more so. He didn't answer immediately, but his expression changed slightly.

"Bees?" he finally said, keeping his eyes on some distant spot across the lake.

"Yeah, you could start a small-scale apiary out in the garden, wear one of those netted suits, and collect the honey . . . that sounds like just your cup of bourbon, doesn't it?"

"Bourbon? Yes, a large one. Thank you."

"How about coffee?" He didn't answer, but I got up and started brewing some anyway. "It could be really interesting to have your own apiary," I went on, keeping an eye on him from the kitchen.

"Apiary," he said quietly. "I think I like the idea of it . . . I do, but . . . "

"But what?"

"There's something just so horrible about the word 'ape.' Why is that?"

"Oh, I think I know what you mean. Is it that sense of the uncanny? Apes are uncannily similar to us, but different enough to make us conscious that they aren't human. You know, shadow creatures living somewhere between the realms of animal and human." It seemed as if Erik might be tempted into a real conversation. Those had been scarce lately, so I did my best to encourage it.

"Well, maybe. Maybe that's the problem." He seemed to be waking up. "That line between human and animal—we fear it, I think. We fear that it may be finer than we'd like to think. We worry about what it might mean. We try so hard, don't we? We try so hard to be distinctly human, but we always end up more like them. It's not a mistake, I think, that we use the word 'ape' to connote pretending—playing a part." This was all very encouraging. I poured our coffee and set a mug on the table in front of Erik.

"Well, I've always thought that particular use of 'ape' was unfair anyway, don't you think so? I mean, it's not as if they pretend to be like us. They *are* like us."

"Yes. Yes, I think that's it. I think that's why we're okay with octopuses."

"Octopuses?" I asked. He looked at me finally and really seemed to see me.

"Octopuses—what should be their heads are actually their bodies—their legs are all arms—their mouths are in their armpits—and their brains wrap around their throats like intelligent turtleneck sweaters." I laughed. This was the first amusing conversation I'd had with him in days. "But it's okay that they're so intelligent," he continued, "—and they are. They're alarmingly intelligent, Elias! But it's okay because they look like aliens. It's hard to picture a creature more different from us. But it's just that degree of difference which makes it okay, even fascinating. But with apes, there is that similarity. It's uncomfortable."

"Why?" I asked. "Why do you think it's uncomfortable?"

"I don't know."

"Maybe it's guilt," I ventured.

"Why guilt?" he asked, finally taking a sip of black coffee.

107

"Well, that we treat them like animals, you know. That they are so similar to us, but we keep them in cages like any other animal at the zoo."

"They say we came from something like them," he said, starting to stuff a pipe.

"Yes. I've heard that as well. Who knows if it's true. But does it matter? I mean, does it really change anything either way?"

"Well, certainly it does," he said, sitting forward, and finally investing himself fully in the conversation. "It could be a reason to discount ancient notions of creation—myths of a young earth—it could explain the brutality of ancient history. Perhaps our species has evolved beyond barbarism, crucifixion, the rack, drawing and quartering . . . "

"Have we though? Have we really?" I asked.

"Well, haven't we? I've never been invited to a hanging or a beheading, have you?"

"No, but we both saw what happened just over the last decade in Vietnam. The massacres, the destruction of humans, animals, trees, and crops. Unspeakable brutality on all sides. Methods have changed, that's all. Technology has changed."

"I don't know about that. I wasn't there. Maybe it's all a lie. The newspapermen can say what they like, and no one ever asks if it's true or not."

"Yeah, I know. But I didn't hear about this on the news. Maybe I missed it, or maybe they did. Honestly, I don't follow it closely. And I wasn't there either. I was meant to be, you know. They called me up, and I went in, but they told me my health was too poor. It seems there may be at least one advantage to having been malnourished as a child if it saved me from conscription."

"Really?" Erik looked me up and down. "I didn't know that about you."

"It doesn't matter. I have the life I have. But I've heard stories from people who were there, you know, in Vietnam. People who came back—saw things—did things. I don't think we've evolved at all in that sense, I mean beyond torture and destruction, from some of the things I've heard. It just keeps happening, but with new tools and new rhetoric to support them."

"So, you think we've always been this way and haven't changed at all? The fossils don't convince you?"

"Oh, I don't know. I suppose it could be true. I almost hope it is. I mean, what a gift! To be raised up into rational thought from some sort of purely reactive existence. But what a responsibility to care for the rest. I mean, to have the burden of reason, language, and skill at fabrication. But all we've reasoned, it seems, are excuses for destruction. And all we've made are cages and walls and new, more efficient weapons. We may have evolved physically . . . I'm still waiting to see us evolve morally."

"Maybe we're all in captivity . . . " Erik mused.

"How do you mean?"

"Like the apes in the zoo. Slaves and captives in a world where hundreds and thousands of years, the thoughts and decisions of others . . . have led us into a way of being and thinking and living that we know is wrong, but which we are helpless to escape. We're branded—stamped out by the particulars of time and space. What can we do? How can we reverse it, or make it right? We can't even change ourselves! We can't even see ourselves, except in the eyes of an ape. We just tend our gardens and write our poetry, trying to feel better while the whole damn world is going up in flames . . . " His voice trailed off.

"But is it wrong to try to feel better? I mean, if you're powerless to change something, what's wrong with at least trying to reach some degree of contentment?" I pursued.

"Take up the violin, you mean?"

"That's not what I'm saying. But don't you think it's okay to try to feel better in some healthy way?"

"Is any form of self-delusion healthy?" He shook his head slowly, then looked at me with something like desperation in his eyes. "Does everyone feel this way?"

"How?"

"Empty—uneasy—estranged—confused—frustrated—isolated—confined. I want happiness, Elias. I want peace. Nothing seems to bring it. Nothing seems to last. Only the dark. The Void."

"Back to the Void again? Will we ever be done with it?" I asked.

"Not until it's done with us. What does it mean? What does it want? Why is it always there—hiding in plain view at the center of everything?"

We looked silently at our coffee. It seemed there were no more words to be said between us. Who knows what it was all for, to begin with? I had gotten him to talk, but all our words had brought us back to the one question that was always there—the one destination of every meandering conversation that came from a place of honesty—the Void. Erik sank back into his paralysis of mind and body, staring at the lake out the window and its black depths.

As the noon hour passed us by in silence, the clouds came in as if from nowhere, obscuring the sun that had shone, sparkling on the lake. Erik finally stirred again and spoke, not looking at me.

"I just thought it would be kind of poetic. But life isn't really poetic, is it? It seems to be, briefly, but all the order and beauty move, like everything else, toward chaos. Isn't that the second law of thermodynamics? That disorder in the universe only increases. Energy only becomes less usable. I feel it's true. I feel my life sucked through time by a force that not only moves it inexorably forward but pulls it apart—steals my heat and light and all motive for action. Entropy. No, life isn't poetic for long. It becomes gray and senseless with all the wrong words or none at all. Pain. Just senseless, wordless pain without limit. And the poetry becomes an illusion, a world of its own distinct from this one, where there is order, predictability, and beauty. But real life is much harsher. Much more severe. And every stanza lived ends in darkness, ambiguity, and question marks. If only life imitated art . . . no, 'I have seen the moment of my greatness flicker
And have seen the eternal Footman hold my coat, and snicker.' . . . Eliot—Prufrock," he explained, noting my expression of confusion.

"I do know that one, actually. I've just never heard you quote another poet before."

"Sometimes it fits." He leaned a little closer to the window and looked up at the sky. "Looks like rain."

"It does. The clouds are coming down."

"Good. I like cloudy days."

"I thought midsummer was your favorite. The sunshine."

"No. Midsummer is just one day trying to make the best of the fact that the sun is shining and that there are people—vacationers, who want to be here on my island. It's just one day to make lemonade, as they say. But when it's overcast and drizzly, the world is as it should be—in tears. It feels more appropriate. The long days of sunshine are just a joke. A mockery. The sun mocks me, Elias."

"You *are* gloomy today! I swear, there's nothing worse than a gloomy poet on a wet day! Why don't you just let it go? Move on and make new order—new beauty. It doesn't have to stay this way, you know. You can find new aspirations." Perhaps I was a little exasperated with him, tiring of his mood, and tiring of his negativity.

"Let it go? Give it up? Move on? To admit it's the end feels like treason—like a massive act of treachery against my old self—against his hard work, ambitions, loves, and ideals. Maybe I'm not him anymore. Maybe I've been many people since he began all this on my behalf. But I feel responsible not to disappoint him. He believed in all of this, and he was happy for a moment. Here comes the rain."

The summer crept along, and I left Erik alone. I gave him his space and stopped pressuring him to talk. I walked alone in the woods or by the lake most of the time, sketching, thinking—only returning to the cottage for food and sleep. Perhaps I shouldn't have left him for so long. Perhaps I had been right to try drawing him out, but the weight of his gloom was heavy to bear, and I wanted to hear birds singing. I hadn't expected to look forward to the garden party, after the incident of the previous year, but a change in conversational partners seemed more and more attractive.

One night toward midsummer, I was awakened by a noise. It was a faint shriek, followed by quick footsteps in the hall and muffled thumping. I peered into the hall and noticed no light, but the air heaved with the sounds of terrified breathing coming from downstairs. I crept down and switched on a lamp to find Erik trying to pour a glass of whiskey, but his hand shook so violently that most of it sloshed onto the rug. He turned to me, startled, with panic in his expression and his whole body shaking uncontrollably.

"What on earth . . . what's going on? Are you okay?" I asked, venturing a little closer.

"Oh, it was horrible! It was . . . it was just the worst, most disgusting . . . ghastly . . . "

"You had a nightmare?"

"Good God! I hope that's all it was! You can't imagine! It was just terrifying! Will you pour me some whiskey? I can't seem to get it in the glass. It's just too horrible!"

"Here, now . . . just a little. Now calm yourself down. It was nothing but a bad dream. It wasn't real . . . it was all in your head. Do you want to talk about it?"

"Oh no, I couldn't. Then you wouldn't sleep either."

"Okay . . . well—"

"I was pregnant! I had a thing growing inside of me. It was a horrible thing. It was an octopus! Or maybe a squid, a giant squid . . . no, yes, I'm sure it was an octopus. It had enormous eyes, and a beak and its suckers were grabbing at my guts!"

"You were pregnant with an octopus?"

"That's not the worst of it!"

"No?"

"No! It gets worse! Much worse!"

"Well?"

"It was my *twin*!"

"Your—"

"Twin! Twin! It was my twin! My twin octopus!"

"You dreamed you were pregnant . . . with your twin octopus."

"I know! I know! It's pure devilry! I shouldn't even have told you. Evil!"

"Well, that's not quite the word I was thinking. What color was it?"

"It was gr— . . . how the devil would I know? It was inside of me! It was grabbing all over with its writhing little tentacles . . . looking for something . . . "

"Mollusks?"

"You think I'm ridiculous! You don't grasp how ominous this is! Ominous! It means something! What does it mean? What does it mean? Why do I even ask you? You don't understand anything! The lake could be boiling blood, and you'd find some reasonable explanation."

"Erik, I do understand. I understand that you had a disturbing dream. Maybe our conversation the other day had something to do with it, remember? You were talking about how smart octopuses are. Octopuses? Octopi?

"Octopodes. That's not it. It was more! It was real!"

"It wasn't real, and you'll be laughing about it in a few hours."

"It wasn't funny! It meant something! It meant something horrible, and I don't want it to be true! It can't be! I don't want it to . . . "

"To what?"

"To kill me! It was looking for my heart to eat it! But why?"

"Maybe you should go back to sleep and find out."

"Don't be stupid. It doesn't work that way. It has to be interpreted. But how? Who can interpret dreams accurately these days without making it all about Mother?"

"Well, I'm going to go back to bed, and maybe I'll dream up an answer for you. Okay?"

"Fine! Go. Sleep. Dream. But don't you mock me! There are more things in heaven and earth, Horatio . . . "

I let him have the last Shakespearean word and left him stewing in his fears and whiskey in an armchair by the encouraging glow of the lamp. I returned to my room and lay awake a few minutes, thinking about my friend and his absurd dream. A smile twisted its way across my face as I whispered "pregnant with his twin octopus" into the darkness. I told myself it was the silliness of the thought that amused me. I would never have allowed myself to believe I was amused by the possibility of my own superiority of mind, or by the idea of his mental deterioration. I couldn't allow any possibilities that made me a villain. About one thing, he was right. There are more things in heaven and earth, more monsters in the microcosm of my own being than I had ever allowed myself to dream.

I awoke the next morning to Erik making phone calls, canceling with guests, photographers, and caterers. He would not risk embarrassing himself after the events of last night. For him, it would be the first time midsummer was canceled—a cruel disappointment, but one he saw no way around. Erik never mentioned the octopus again, and I didn't ask. The remainder of the summer would drag along quietly, with both good days and bad days, until I boarded the ferry to the mainland, telling myself he was much improved thanks to my wholesome influence and continuous care.

Tucked in the eastern-facing corner of the old cottage, there hung an oil lamp. It always seemed to be burning. Babushka made sure of that. In the evenings, the shimmering orange glow from the lamp made the faces in the icons that hung on the wall look as though they moved—as though their expressions were changing ever so slightly if you watched them vigilantly. And the little boy did watch them. He would sit by Babushka's feet some evenings while she worked with her needle and thread to repair his torn trousers or Dedushka's socks, just watching the moving faces of the saints in the corner. He liked them. They seemed alive, sometimes stern, sometimes laughing, but always truly present with him. His favorite was a man in armor, holding a long spear and riding a white horse. It looked as though the horse was trampling a fierce, writhing dragon underfoot.

"Babushka, was Saint George a real person?" the little boy asked one winter evening.

"Yes, of course, my joy. Of course, Saint George is real."

"Did he really kill a dragon?"

"Kill? No, he didn't kill it. He only wounded it so that it would learn to be a good, obedient dragon who would be a guardian and protector, instead of a wicked beast that only wanted to hurt people."

"So, dragons are real? Dragons and monsters really exist?"

"Of course, dear. We see them all the time."

"I've never seen one."

"If you live long enough, you will."

"Are you sure they really exist?" the boy asked skeptically. Babushka laid down her needle and thread, smoothing the little boy's mended trousers over her lap. She laid a wrinkled hand on his head.

"Dragons and monsters are not animals you might find in a cave in the forest. You can't see them, at least not as they truly are. They often like to disguise themselves as something good and natural, if they let you see them at all."

"But, you said they were real . . . "

"Yes, it's true. They are quite real. They exist in each of us, my love. They are the evil thoughts and ideas that cause men to wage war, to torture and kill one another, to commit mindless destruction of living things. They are the evil thoughts that cause us to do wrong to each other."

"So, they aren't real . . . " the little boy said with a sigh of disappointment.

"But they are! And much more dangerous than you can imagine! Someday you will see one. Maybe it will be making its home in you—in your heart—and you will have a choice whether to let it stay, ignore it and call it a dream, or whether to fight it until you've made it good and obedient to you. Life is full of such choices. Sometimes it's so confusing—like when you find that you've done the right thing for the wrong reason. Bad motives are like dragons whispering in your heart."

They sat quietly again, only the crackle of the stove, and the groan of the cottage in the winter wind filled the silence. The little boy stared into the saints' faces in the corner. The lamplight shivered when a draft from the window slipped through the casing and disturbed its stillness. He imagined himself as a valiant knight on a white horse. No evil dragon could ever make its home in his brave heart.

If only we could stay children, honest and brave, and never grow up to be monsters.

10

Winter is Coming

WHY IS IT CALLED *"value?" Really, why? I don't mean this hypothetically, as though I'm asking a question I already know the answer to and am just pedantically setting the stage for an impressive exposé on the word's etymology. That's Erik's game. I have such struggles with words and their meanings. Maybe because I remember learning these words for the first time, as a child who already owned two other extensive vocabularies for most of the essential things one needs to say in life, or perhaps I would ask these questions regardless of my linguistic background. But I'm not insane for asking. I may be insane for other reasons, but this isn't one of them.*

In art, value has to do with degrees of light and shadow, like high and low keys on a scale. But why call it "value" at all? As though by darkening a canvas, increasing values, you are actually increasing its worth. Doubtless for Tenebrists and other practitioners of "the dark manner" in baroque era painting, pushing values to the lowest keys and making them instruments of exaggerated emotion, did think increased value equated increased worth. I like Chiaroscuro. Moreover, I very much like Caravaggio. However, there's a time and a place—a context for everything in art. Surely there are moments when decreased values may prove, for lack of a better word, more valuable.

Why, why, why is it called "value?" Push those values; deepen those values; increase those values. How many times did I hear those words bandied about like they really meant something during art critiques? It's what you say when you don't know what to say. But some take it all so deadly serious, courting the darkness, seeing how far they can go into the Void before turning chicken and beating it back to bright. In the end, you can experiment and play philosopher all you like, but the answer comes down to the needs of the subject and the motive of the work as a whole. It may prove true that without the darkness, those increased values, we lose our sense of space—of dimensionality. We may even lose our sense of reality if reality was the goal. A canvas—a world, even—without darkness, without shadows and glooming pools appears flat and meaningless to the eye, if only because our sad reality is full of them. Can I even imagine a world without darkness?

Darkness is necessary for shaping space and defining form but is rarely the subject in and of itself. Unless, like the late abstract expressionist whose work I have known and loved, one delights so much in the low-key values, that one produces whole fields of profound and impenetrable blacks that become the subjects themselves. I remember I cried when I learned of his suicide a few years ago—diving, as it were, finally into the shadows and glooming pools of darkness which he had translated as best he could on canvas. He courted the darkness more passionately than I have ever dared.

So yes, value is indeed valuable, but in terms of worth, darkness must be considered equal to light, at least in the ability to suggest form and texture, indeed, to set the entire mood of the piece. We need both, or else we succumb to that despair which comes from looking so long into the Void that we lose hope that light exists at all—or so long at the light that our mental eye is scorched by its purity. Either way, at some point, you have to blink. You have to back away and have a cup of tea.

Oh, I have these thoughts, but my brain is too puny for them! Who knows if they hold any value . . . in the sense of being worth the time it takes to think them and jot them down in my diary as if they are so very necessary to remember. But I have watched every day as the leaves of the maple tree on the corner have lost their healthy summer green and have become first tinged at the edges then gradually, and now entirely, overtaken by reds of ever-deepening value. Value can be harder to judge chromatically. Achromatic values are easy enough, but when life around us, in full color, dazzles us with its brilliance, we notice the change in color, but not always the change in value. We know a change is occurring because we see the greens fading and reds deepening, but how often do we fail to notice that the darkness is closing in?

I've watched this tree change. It has been like watching a piece of paper catch fire, slowly at first along the edge until the entire surface flames and curls. The result is the same: terribly beautiful while it lasts, only to give way to crumbling ashes and brittle skeletons that scrape and scuttle over the pavement when the wind blows. So how will I be any different? How are any of us *any different from the changing leaves? We all know where this is heading at last, and one could do so much worse than to blaze brightly for a brief moment before returning to feed the flowers. Yes, one would do well to die like a leaf, to live a life of deepening value, and finally to go up in flames.*

I have heard that leaves don't actually change color in autumn, at least not essentially. The tree simply stops feeding them, and they return to the shade they've always been underneath the verdant masquerade of health and youth—of growth and life. It's only when the leaves have reached the end of their life that their true colors show through—nothing to hide. I wonder if I will be so honest in death. Honest and yet still beautiful. Perhaps, like the oak, I'll find that I was only ever brown, and I'll cling stubbornly to the tree all winter, refusing to move on. But I may burn fiercely red. One can hope.

It is sad, watching things die. Even the beauty of the autumn maple on the corner simply serves as a reminder that nothing lasts forever, and the values only ever deepen. I do love the fall, though, short as it is. It does seem to be the best of seasons. "Live every day in remembrance of your death," my babushka once said to me. Probably she said it more than once since I remember it. But why? Why not live in perpetual springtime—at least believing, or choosing to believe that your life will never end? Oh, but it will, and sooner than you think, I almost hear her say. Remember that every moment is the moment of your death and learn not to despair. Yes, perhaps she said that as well. The trees—the deepening values of the seasons—won't allow me to forget my own death, but maybe one day it won't frighten me so very much.

I do feel it very strongly today, in the air, the spicy smell of dying leaves, in the silent withering of late flowers, in the changing quality of the light—the deepening values from the pale sunlight of the young year to the russet light of autumn. Yes, I feel it. Winter is coming.

11

Notes from the Underground

As I WALK THE streets of this city, I feel its breath; I sense its quick, rhythmic heartbeat; I hear its hungry groaning. I walk into its gaping mouth and then its rumbling belly: the subway. This city in the cold dead of winter feeds on souls. With every breath I take, I feel my soul drawn from me, my chest tightening painfully to prevent its theft. With every breath exhaled, I fancy I see my diaphanous essence float up in white, frosty clouds. It's just a lot of hot air, I tell myself. I'm just a lot of hot air. A pretender. A child playing at being an artist. The reason I don't have exhibitions isn't that I'm waiting until I have a worthy portfolio. It's because I know I'll be found out. They'll see I'm out of my depth, and I'm not what I'm advertising. I'm just another philistine and a dilettante who can't manage to paint the portrait of a goddess.

My work is nothing special or new. Art is everywhere in New York City. It is as much in the subway as the Metropolitan, though the contents of this city's belly are seldom examined, let alone praised by critics. It is the brash, illicit art of the oppressed. Saying the uncomfortable, and portraying the basest realities on a public platform, jolting us to look and see, to feel our human frailty, here in the shadows of the underground, rather than to soothe and silence old fears in the pleasant warmth of the sunlit museum galleries.

I think that is what the avant-garde has tried to do, in its own self-conscious way, to mixed success. They try to make their little experiences of pain speak for humanity in ways unheard of in polite circles. Yes, they can make a little suffering go a long way—spreading it thinly, sparingly. But the voices of poverty, of the real grit and pain of everyday living, won't find themselves in museums or art history courses, lauded as the brave souls who triggered some important paradigm shift. Their suffering isn't cultivated and pragmatically utilized; it comes too near the abyss. They touch its darkness, live on the brink of it, and make us squirm uncomfortably with tasteless portrayals. If we must acknowledge the Void, some protest, can we not avoid vulgarity and approach it with some delicacy? That's my problem. I'm too delicate.

I, for one, believe these dark claims, these whispers, and graffiti. I believe some have seen monsters and demons in the darkness, even if I haven't seen the same ones. But I haven't yet given up hope that there may be beauty as well. After all, value is a scale, and if darkness cannot exist without light, then demons cannot exist without angels. Moreover, the capacity to worship cannot exist without the existence of something worth worshipping. At least I choose to hope, and hope is not delicate. Hope demands a ruggedness and resilience of soul far beyond what despair requires of us.

As I approach my easel this snowy night, my mind is full both with the fears and the shadows of the winter underground, and the hope and beauty of the golden midsummer light which I hold in my memory like a precious flame which I must shelter from the chill intrusion of the wind. I cling to the hope that I can learn to surpass my classroom-cultivated skills and finally paint the portrait of a goddess. I sketch her now-familiar form in gesture on my canvas. I find it easier to draw her now. I accept the reality of those cruel and unapologetic shadows knowing that they imply the light and its source and that she is complexly defined by both in conflict. This is true; at least I think it must be—that the one gives evidence of the other—that it is this conflict which rounds out our flat forms. This is true. This is human.

12

Negative Space

NO PIECE OF ART can be judged on the beauty of shapes and forms alone, and by shapes and forms, I mean the positive image. Certainly, these positive spaces are the first things the viewer notices—the fullness, the tangible substance of what appears to be the subject. Some of us will never progress beyond the admiration of positive space and what appears to be actual. It takes a shift in perspective to recognize that for every form, there is a hollow—for every fullness a concavity—for every presence and absence—that every form we observe is shaped and defined by the Void. It is only by the invisible force of what is not that we can see what truly is.

I can appreciate the Rococo to a degree, as a movement defined by the intense desire to fill the negative space, decorating it with ornate embellishments. Empty spaces create unease as if we sense the analogy of physical and spiritual void. You could call the Rococo an artistic movement devoted to filling holes or at least distracting us from them. The negative is a lonely desert place.

To finally accept the negative space in a picture is to finally accept the negative space in the subject herself. Her embellished form, however distracting, is itself defined by its relationship to the negative space which exposes inner surfaces, if only we dare explore them. It is the knowledge of these inner voids, the knowledge of her humanity, hints of its weakness, frailty and insecurity, that has finally made her visible and therefore paintable to me. Perhaps the answer has always been that painting a goddess is impossible, but painting a person is not. I know a little better now what I'm seeing.

I paint her now, a negative form, a blank space fully enveloped in tangible, positive darkness. The darkness itself becomes the subject, the real and concrete, and she is only a hollow in that glooming mass which bears down, feeling every surface of her absent form. It is desolate and tragic, a form defined only as an absence.

I cannot apologize for loving beautiful forms. However, in shifting perspective, to see the invisible forces which define them, the concavities that hide secrets both beautiful and hideous, I have learned to see both in concert. She is no mere form and no mere absence. She is a complex being of light and shadow, of form and hollow, of fullness and concavity who has placed herself in the center of that crushing Void. She is human.

13

The Third Dimension

I've NEVER BEEN FLUENT *in the third dimension. That fact gives me a real sense of grief and even embarrassment as an artist. I've appreciated it, admired the triumphs of others who have mastered space to this degree. When I have tremulously dug my fingers into the cold block of clay to release a captive bird from a solid, earthen mass, I have found myself clumsy, only ever having the smallest of success with relief. I made an ear once—a somewhat abstract ear cast in plaster relief. And very shallow relief at that. But how I would love, as Michelangelo, to set prisoners free! Prisoners frozen in cold, white marble, just waiting . . . waiting for the right pair of eyes to gaze upon the faceless block and see what hides inside. Oh, to hew away that solid prison! To chip and chisel and polish! To be able to physically circumnavigate one's own work and see it from behind, from beneath—to reach inside it and feel the hollows. Not just to see forms but feel them. How I envy sculptors.*

I've tried. Of course I've tried. I was required to try, and I was only told what I already knew: that my best work was in two dimensions—the flat plane. I've often wondered why. Could it be a small failure . . . such as a lack of discipline or practice? Or is it more? Why? Unless it points to some defect in my capacity to see and grasp the world as anything but flat. Beautiful. Yes, quite beautiful, but flat. I'm told I should never think of two-dimensional art as superior or inferior to three-dimensional art, that the two are merely different. However, it still stings in that tender little prideful part of an artist's soul, to have mastered one and possess absolutely no knack for the other.

I've longed to manipulate space and finally see what is behind and underneath my forms. Even to look inside and see the Void expanding ever outward within one weak and feeble form. Perhaps she was right that one summer, my photographic zealot. I think of her often and most of all the things she said about me. Perhaps my perspective is limited. I can't manipulate space and show the many perspectives of a subject because I can see only one: my own. Perhaps it's true, but I could have sworn, as an artist, I had a gift for seeing.

How I wish I understood space and dimensions. I mean really understood them, but it's so mathematical, and I'm sure that's part of the problem. What sense can mathematics possibly make to a man who grew up thinking numbers were persons—persons with their own colors and relationships with each other, completely independent of actual color theory. Of course, 3 and 5 must never be combined. 3 is in love with 4 and 4 is in love with 3. 5 would ruin 3's delicate lilac color with its brash, primary red, and would consume it entirely. 3 would cease to exist, being lost to 5's color and personality. 4, on the other hand, only enhances 3, and three enhances 4. 4 makes 3 a little deeper. 3 makes 4 a little lighter. They should be together. It's right for them to be together. Together they make 7, which is all verdant green and perfection in every way. Let 5 find someone else to pair with—perhaps another prime primary. Such is the curse of being an imaginative child who was too much alone. Oh, the worlds we create for ourselves and the rules we impose on reality. Reality itself only gets in the way and interferes, making everything that ugly middle gray.

Oh, but how I wish I understood dimensionality, I mean beyond the rudimentary. I perceive that the third and fourth dimensions are the ones that matter most—the inner spaces and the directionality of time. Yet I return from any adventure in spacetime to my planar understanding of things. The frustration of knowing that whole universes of meaning exist in that one concept I can't quite master! If only I was a sculptor. Or a physicist. To open up my understanding of space and time, or rather explode it! If only.

No, my most significant claim is that I can achieve the illusion of space and depth through tricks of value and scale on a two-dimensional plane. In that, at least, I'm fluent—in giving the impression of profound depths—but on closer inspection, it's just a lot of pretty subterfuge. Isn't that an age-old saying? I feel like I heard long ago that every depth has a surface, but not all surfaces have a depth. I missed my calling by a few hundred years. What a living I might have made painting trompe l'oeil for the French aristocracy! Look at my work! The pretty surface is all there is, and behind, beneath, within, there is nothing!

14

Forced Perspective and the Simulacrum

SOMETIMES IT FEELS I'VE *been waiting my entire life to learn a particular word. I've been searching for it indirectly, feeling its existence lurking in the penumbra of my consciousness, a creature of half-light. The day when the word is spoken to me, or I read it in a book, I know that I've found it even before I've consulted my dictionary to make sure it means what I think it means. And it does! The word exists, and there is finally a verbal expression to give voice to that nagging, non-discursive presence which has been little more than a dry seed in my brain, dormant, waiting for its moment—for symbolic representation in language. It feels like I've discovered a new continent or an element or something similarly grand. Never mind that people have been using the word for centuries, and I, in my ignorance, have only stumbled upon it by accident.*

I felt that way when I learned the Latin word "simulacrum." I read it first, then I said it aloud. I said it over and over, though there was no one but me to hear it. Simulacrum . . . simulacrum. I whispered it: simulacrum. I obsessed over the way it felt in my mouth, and it rang with deafening silence in my ears when I was busy with other things. It felt ominous, dark, threatening, and deceitful. This is the word for which I've been at a loss. This is the meaning I haven't been able to speak. Now I've been given the gift of a word, so I'll share it if writing it down in my diary can be considered "sharing." I have no one else to tell it to, but at least this way I'll remember it.

On the surface level, I believe this word means simulation or an imitation of something real. If that was all it meant, then Plato, Nietzsche, Baudrillard, and Deleuze wouldn't have pressed the point. It seems that what one believes about this haunting word, means a great deal for how one defines reality and its structure.

How you used to drop names
and pretend to know things.

Instances in the Latin Vulgate have been translated as "idol," which may or may not be helpful, depending on how one defines an "idol." If I define "idol" as simulation, statue, or representation, there is little to fear, and less to seriously contemplate. Who will fear a naked, marble Greek, modestly fig-leafed by the Victorians, with pupils gouged out in negative, and a crumbling nose? But inherent to the word "idol" is the suggestion of worship, which is not a part of the general definition of "simulacrum." However, it is this implication that takes the word simulacrum to its darkest place.

Naturally, I understand "simulacra" best through art and its theory. Forced perspective illustrates it rather well, I think. When forced perspective is in use, this form of optical illusion can convince the viewer that he or she is looking down a hallway 100 meters long, viewing a massive gilded age mansion situated on a lake, or looking at a giant human being the size of a tyrannosaurus rex. It only works when the viewer is standing in—or the photo is taken from—the correct spot. These are distortions, but not complete fabrications. The hallway, the mansion, the giant all exist, but perspective has forced them to appear to be something they are not. The remedy to believing the distortion instead of the reality may be as simple as taking a few steps to the side, viewing the subject from a different angle. In doing this, one may be astonished by the truth: that the 100-meter hallway is a painted wall, that the enormous mansion on a lake is a doll's house next to a puddle, that the giant is, in fact, a dwarf among his peers.

How often are our idols, our simulacra, so diabolically subtle? While it seems ridiculous to bow in worship to a fig-leafed marble Greek, how natural, unconscious even, to worship a particular perspective—an angle on reality that is forced and distorted. If only we could get around to the other side of our perceptions, circumnavigate our ideas, our beliefs, our friends . . . ourselves. To see things as they truly are instead of how we are told to see them.

Do you think you could bear it?

15

Color Theory

I KNOW NEXT TO nothing about color theory and less about optics. This is to my shame as an artist. Whether I was hungover or just daydreaming in that class, I came away with very little beyond the impression that color and our perception of it is a lot more scientific than I was comfortable with at the time. I do know a little about the color wheel: primaries, secondaries, tertiaries . . . the more you mix and combine, the more alike they all become until finally, you end your journey through the colors at a perfectly flat grey. They're all people and personalities, of course, colors are, and vice versa—meaning people, their personalities, suggest certain colors. I see them on my palette, and I feel I know them intimately, those brash, bold primaries so sure of themselves and uncompromising. They have nothing to hide. The secondaries are equally secure in their identities, but they are much more flexible. Being the blended offspring of two such bold and opposing personalities, they become something new and curious, yet entirely understandable in their natures. I am a tertiary, an earthy neutral composed of so many conflicting colors, thoughts, and attributes—teetering on the edge of an ambiguous grayscale, clinging to the many identities blended up within me. I don't know them all, but when I see myself in a certain light, I sometimes become aware of colors in my soul that I never knew existed.

I sit silently in my chartreuse armchair and light my pipe, something I've picked up from Erik. I've given up cigarettes. I like the image, the ethos of pipe-smoking. I tell myself that, but in all practicality, it's a cheaper habit to keep and I've begun to suspect my lungs are unhealthy. The cavern of my jaws fills with spicy aromatic smoke, which spills from my lips in that perfect gray that is the blended presence of all colors. My mind wanders, flooded with colors and textures and moods. A scene is setting itself, flickering like a film projected on the wall at which I stare in silence. Act one; scene one. Enter: A man. Frail. Tired. Emaciated. Stinking of vodka and vomit. He crawls on his hands and knees. It's Erik. This isn't reality, though. In fact, it's rather an ugly image I've conjured up—just one of the thousands of seedy images that have come to constitute my darkening soul. Should I blow the smoke away? Should I switch off the projector? Brush away the mental image like a fly? Think of Christmas, or roses, or wild mushrooms? Maybe I should, but what harm would it do to entertain the thought for the duration of a pipe? Thoughts are only thoughts, after all. They can harm no one.

I enter the scene again. Erik—the bold, the brash, the confident, primary red—has faded to gray. His body is wracked with convulsions of sickness; his eyes are darkening, looking up at me. I'm glowing primary yellow, like the sun. I never knew I was that color. He reaches up toward me, weakly. But I'm too high for him to reach, and he is slipping lower. Freja saunters into the picture—old, haggard, as gray and flat as Erik. She postures herself preposterously, still expecting to be looked at, and still expecting to be admired. She looks as though she is actually trying to seduce me; her chin dipped coquettishly. But she, too, is fading away and slipping further into the darkness. The lower they sink, the higher and brighter I become. It's as though I'm absorbing their colors—their life force.

This thought is awfully bizarre—horrendous even. I really ought to send it away and think of something else . . . candles, stars, trackless expanses of snow . . . but I feel such a thrill, an electric charge of excitement as I continue to watch my mental cinema, and after all, thoughts are insubstantial. They're all in my head. What harm can they do? Who would even know?

Erik's skin is sagging now, loose like crepe. He tears at his face and arms with his fingers, and the skin comes off in his hands. He is succumbing to corruption—decomposing—screaming now in agony. His eyes are sinking deep into his skull. Freja's breasts are dry and shriveled like a mummy, her nose has fallen away, and her sagging skin is covered in rotting holes. She places a hand on her hip and poses for me grotesquely as if she still believes she's still quite beautiful. I continue to rise above them, into the sky. I'm glowing yellow, so bright now that they can't bear to look at me, and they continue to become smaller, darker, more hideous and deformed until they fade away to nothing.

My pipe has gone out. I tap out the ashes. The world has come back, and the room is heavy with gray smoke. The winter day is ending, and I hear the scratching, shuffling feet of pigeons huddled in the rain gutter above the window. The room has desaturated, become colorless since sunset. Even my chartreuse chair is gray in the twilight. I would never hurt them. I would never do anything to hurt them. Thoughts are strange things. Who knows where they come from or what they mean, or why they make us feel the way they do. But I would never do anything to harm them. That is not what my thoughts mean. It's not what they mean at all. I don't know what they mean. It doesn't matter anyway. Thoughts are insubstantial. Ineffectual. They can do nothing. They can injure no one.

Mind your thoughts, Eliasz.
Mind—your—thoughts.

I don't want to want these things. I don't understand it. I just sat down in my chair—I stuffed a pipe—I lit it, twice, and finally got it glowing in the twilight. It just came on its own; I didn't invite it. I don't believe it was even mine, to begin with.

Even if it wasn't,
You suffered it to stay.
That was your first mistake.

It didn't mean anything. It was nothing.

How you have mocked
yourself with such lies.

I hope . . . that is, I will try to forget these ugly thoughts, which I've looked at for too long. Yes, I admit that I did. I looked too long. But I will forget. They will be nothing. They are nothing. I'm just too sensitive. I am really far too sensitive. Maybe it's that I'm too much alone. But why should it matter if I indulge in silly thoughts over a pipe on a winter's evening? Is a man to deny himself all luxury? Who's to judge? What is a thought anyway? Where does it come from? Why should I regret something that has no tangible reality? I don't want to want these things; in fact, I'm sure I don't. It's not what I want at all. It's just a puff of smoke, soon to blow away. There. It's gone.

I was a fool; I am still a fool.
I have grown old and learned a little,
but the agony remains:
I have wanted the wrong things
and gotten them.

PART III—1976

1

1976

I DIDN'T FEEL THE same lightheartedness on the ferry crossing the Strait of Juan de Fuca that summer of 1976. The view was the same, but my attitude had changed. I imagined the peaceful seascape of tree-covered islands and swooping seagulls, now obscured in a silent mist, being suddenly swallowed whole down the dark, jagged gullet of a Cascade Range turned predatory, stalking like whitetip sharks on the southern horizon. I felt in my gut that something was coming. My last conversations with Erik had made me feel sorry for him. I had never thought it was possible to pity Erik, but he was crumbling around the edges, losing his strength and his sharpness. He was still my friend, but I wasn't looking forward to seeing him, fearing the state in which I might find him and the awkwardness of his despondency. It was possible he would be back to his old self—healthy and robust, at peace with Freja and their future, or at least moving on to an alternate future. I hoped, but I didn't dare expect to find them both happy.

The ferry carried me onward into this ambiguous future, as vague as the horizon cloaked in fog. I sat inside, felt no movement of wind, and glanced unseeing out the window. When I arrived at the terminal, I was surprised to see Freja waiting, as beautiful as usual. She gave me a nod of recognition when she saw me, as though I hadn't been away for months but only an hour or two. I tried to shake off my surprise, agonizing briefly over whether a hug was the appropriate greeting, and deciding just to smile and try not to seem uncomfortable.

"Erik is sleeping. You might have waited all day for him here, so I came instead."

"Is he okay?" I asked. She smiled faintly and gestured.

"The car is this way."

I was tempted to try for a pleasant conversation with Freja in the car, but I couldn't think of anything interesting to say, and rather than appear as foolish as I felt, I said nothing. She was quiet and disengaged until, without preliminaries, as if our last (and first) real conversation had never quite ended, she spoke.

"It didn't work, you know. Whatever you said to him, I think it just upset him more."

"Oh, really? I'm sorry. I was sure he was coming around when I left."

"Coming around?"

"You know, I thought he was changing his mind about wanting a child. We had some conversation where he seemed to be, you know, disappointed, but at least starting to resign himself. I thought he might be starting to think differently."

"He does think differently now."

"I thought you said—"

"He thinks he needs more booze—as if he wasn't already saturated! He thinks his health and his sanity aren't even worth preserving anymore. You were right about resigning himself. He has resigned, he has retired . . . he has weighted his better judgment down with rocks and drown it in the lake!"

"Oh . . . "

"He's ruining himself. He couldn't become a father now even if he tried, and he knows it. At least he can only blame himself now, not me. I'm safe in that sense. He need never know . . . " Her voice trailed off as though she were talking to herself. I stared silently at the road, embarrassed, during a pause that I felt powerless to fill. She glanced back at me finally. "You're uncomfortable. But you should know what you're going to see. He's wrecked himself, and he knows it. What's more, he doesn't even seem to care anymore. Still, he's tremendously fragile."

"I'm so sorry, Freja," and I really thought I was. Anyway, what else could I say?

"It can't go on like this. He's falling apart. It's more than a nervous breakdown—nervous, physical—if he doesn't come back to himself soon, I'll . . . I suppose I could do it again. I hadn't intended to, but maybe it's not too late for me. Maybe I still have time to find someone else and make a new start." She seemed to be talking to herself again.

"Oh, don't say that! You two are made for each other. I'll think of something. I promise."

"Elias, I'm sorry to put this on you. You're a good person, and you don't deserve to be in the middle, but I don't know who else to ask. Can't you talk to him again? Try to talk him out of this hell he's made for himself, maybe from a different angle this time?"

"I'm not sure I can say anything that will help. I think it's more than disappointment about not having a son. It's like he's seen, for the first time, that he's not a god, and life isn't an epic poem. Am I supposed to talk him back into believing something that was never true?" She stabbed me with an indignant gaze.

"What's worse? To believe a fairytale, or to die choking on your own vomit . . . or worse, by your own hand?"

"You don't think he would . . . "

"Please, Elias. Just talk to him."

"Freja, there are just no words." We paused, both staring through the windshield at the road as it curved ahead.

"Then do something," Freja finally said.

"Do? What can I possibly do?" Freja stared ahead like a statue, perfectly sculpted, expressionless, like the marble goddess who greeted me on my first evening in the San Juan Islands, two years ago. My mind began entertaining the seed of an idea. It erupted in scope until my mind was nearly euphoric with the possibility. It was as if I'd been waiting for it my whole life, and it had to be.

"He can still see," I said. She looked at me blankly a moment and beckoned me to continue. "Freja, I could paint you. I could paint you for him."

"How is that going to help?"

"It'll be glorious! Mythical! It can be the fairytale image of a lifetime! Something better, more inspiring than all those photographs he keeps of you in his room. You know what I think of photography. Give me a chance to do it right."

"This isn't the time or the place for you to indulge your pet theories. Our marriage . . . our lives are at stake."

"Exactly. He needs to be rescued from his . . . disillusionment. He needs to be reminded of your beauty and that you are all he needs. He needs to be drawn back into the poem. I'll paint you for him, inspire him, flatter him a little. Maybe if he sees you and the life you could have together through fresh eyes, immortalized on canvas, he'll step back into the scene himself. I'll make it a midsummer gift for him . . . and for you." Freja silently considered for a moment that seemed to last an eternity. To my mind, it was the hand of fate, the perfect denouement to their narrative, and my own chance at greatness. It had to be.

"Maybe," she said at last, and I released the breath I'd been unconsciously holding in silence. "The photographs have made him happy in the past until that little backstabber thought she'd try to be clever and nearly ruined years of work. You do have talent. Okay. Do it. Make it good. Make it your best." She paused and pierced me with her grey eyes. "But I won't sit for you. There's no need. I know you've drawn me before." I stammered some embarrassed contradiction, but there was no denying that I had a portfolio of studies to work from. Since my first summer with them, I hadn't drawn anything else. As we finally approached the cottage, my mind was teeming with ideas and images.

2

My Hero

WHEN WE ARRIVED, ERIK stumbled out to meet me and flung his arms around me in a weak, reeky embrace. He took me to the deck and sat silently next to me, looking blankly ahead. Erik had grown increasingly inward-focused since I'd left him the year before. He had come to neglect his physique; a softness had developed about his girth, and his face and neck seemed puffy. Even his skin had taken on a yellowish, glistening pallor. He wasn't well. His loneliness was made apparent in a new tendency to talk to himself audibly, mumbling to himself between silences and barely acknowledging my presence. During these disturbing moments, he staged between himself and the imagined other the exhumation of old arguments, remorseful apologies, and fantastical reconciliations. He was bleeding inwardly, and those sporadic dialogues were evidence of his emotional hemorrhage.

I listened. I watched his moist, puffy lips dribble spirits down his stubbled chin. It was only when I shifted uncomfortably in my chair that he remembered my presence.

"She avoids me, you know. She doesn't eat with me or talk with me or touch me, or anything. She knows me, you see. She knows me. She sees everything, judges everything, and she rejects everything. She rejects me! But it's not my fault! It's not! It can't be! But who's to blame? I don't know . . . I don't know! Circumstance, fate . . . I don't know. But it's not my fault! We were happy! But now she rejects me!"

I listened. I watched his moist, puffy eyes dribble tears down his stubbled cheek. I simply sat, watched, and listened until he forgot my presence again. Eventually, he stumbled down to the shore and lay in his canoe. I didn't follow.

She avoided him, it was true, but that was nothing new. However, she didn't leave him entirely either, a mystery that confounded my brain as I stared at the lake to the background of distant gasps and sobs. Why didn't she leave him—an ailing, babbling man who used to be, at least seemingly, both physically and intellectually colossal, but now lay weeping unrestrainedly in his canoe, consuming his broken spirit in spirits of grain? Why continue making each other miserable, leaving each other to be consumed by jealousy and grief? It seemed that a terrible need existed between them—a need for worship. He was still a slave to her beauty, but what could have kept her there? It's one thing to be worshipped by a robust and handsome intellectual who writes poetry by firelight, commanding the respect of both peers and critics. It's quite another to be worshipped by a stinking, weeping wreck of a man plummeting headfirst into the abyss of madness.

I left him there in the canoe when it was clear that he had drifted into sleep. I wandered back into the house and met Freja coming out of her room.

"My God, do you see what's happening to him?" I whispered. "I had no idea he was so bad. I'm not sure a painting will do much at this point. Don't you think it might be better if you just let each other move on and find happiness elsewhere?" She looked at me long and hard before answering.

"Do you even know what's happening?" she asked. "You don't, do you? You're completely confused. All you see is a great man who is killing himself for no good reason—some dramatic fool who can't weather a little disappointment—and you think I'm just standing by and letting it happen. You think if we called the whole thing off, everything would just go back to normal . . . he'd recover. You don't understand worship." She put her hand on my shoulder and squeezed hard. "It's too late! It's simply too late! It was too late back then when we began. It was ending even as we were starting! It could have ended any number of ways, but it had to end eventually. In the end, a sacrifice is necessary. I could have sacrificed my beauty for a child— the child he wanted. Did you know I was ready? But sometimes you're only ready when it's too late. It's been so long . . . so very, very long, and it's later than you think. I would have been ready to sacrifice my beauty, hoping that even if I couldn't get it back fully, he might still worship its memory and be well again. But even if I could have a child, he has utterly destroyed himself over the belief that I have been simply unwilling. I couldn't hope to find another again at this point. Not like this. I was ready to make the sacrifice, but it was too late. Now the sacrifice is his to make. He's not a victim, Elias. He's finally paying his tithe; that is the cost of worship."

"But can't you ease his suffering a little?"

"And how would I do that? Sleep with him? Remind him of his impotence? Sit and listen to his crazy talk when there's nothing I can say to him that will help? This suffering is his right—even his free choice. I can hardly believe that you know so little about worship. Worship is suffering—sometimes exquisite, other times horrific, but worship is always painful. Worship is a slow death to the worshipped one, and there are only ever palliatives. Give a dying man some comfort. Give him a portrait of his goddess. Let him see his pain as a privilege. I won't leave him while he's still breathing, but that's the best I can do for him now."

"Is it, though? Freja, you know my painting isn't going to make him well . . . not for good."

"I can't turn back time, Elias. I can't fix him, but is it right to deny a lame man a crutch? Let him believe for a moment that everything is okay. Let him feel for a moment that it hasn't all been a waste. Paint that portrait well and feel comforted that you gave a lame man a crutch."

3

The Unraveling

The sun was smiling down warmly on the day they planted Papa, like a seed in the garden. The little boy was confused; he didn't know how to feel. The day was so cheerful and warm, with birds singing and just a whisper of a breeze. It felt unnatural to be sad, but he knew he was. He must be. Yes, he must be very sad, indeed. He hadn't known what it meant to be very sad until now. Mama didn't cry. Her face was like stone as she stood there in the cemetery, holding his hand a little too tight. How long must they have stood in the cemetery staring at that heap of loam? They sang Memory Eternal, ate the sweet, boiled grains, and not once did he see Mama's face change, but that night he heard her, and he knew she was sad like him.

The little boy was curled up sleeping with a blanket by the stove, holding onto the big orange cat, when he awoke with a sudden surge of panic. His heart knocked against the walls of his chest. His head burned like a torch. He gasped for air as though he were drowning, and he *was* drowning. The sudden realization of loss crashed over his head like a wave, dragging him through terrifying depths. Papa wasn't coming back. Papa was gone, and life would never be the same. This terror squeezed him from the inside, and he began to shake violently. The cat, disturbed by the boy's trembling, left him alone, all by himself. Impelled as if by some force, he rose to his feet and hobbled to his mother's bedside.

"Mama, I'm shaking, and I can't stop. I'm not cold, but I'm shaking so hard!" Mama pulled her little boy into bed next to her and held him close. She ran her fingers through his hair and kissed his cheek. Still, he shook uncontrollably.

"My boy, my boy. You're sad, and it's right to be sad, but you have to know that everything will be okay. With time, I promise, everything will be okay. Maybe we won't stay here. Maybe it will be too painful. Maybe we'll make a break and start life someplace new, just you and me. Someplace without so many memories. Lots of people are making good lives for themselves in America. Maybe we'll go there, just you and me. We'll forget this place and everything that makes us sad and get away. Everything will be new and clean, and we'll both be happy again."

The little boy started to doze off as his trembling finally subsided. He didn't hear all that Mama said to him that night. She kept whispering to him, but just the sound of her whisper and the warmth of her arms lulled him to sleep. He knew now, at least, that it was right to be sad. He needn't fear it. Everything would be okay.

"Sleep, Eliasz. Everything will be okay. You'll see."

I like to think of myself as an honest man, but I know that's only wishful thinking. Of all the lies I've told in my life, the one that goes "it's all right—everything's going to be okay" seems the most recurrent, smearing its way across the canvas of my conscience in a shocking motif. I've been told that lie myself more times than I care to remember, and often I believed it. It was my choice to believe it. It's easier to carry on with at least a pretense of hope, and I've helped others deceive themselves as well. I am not really an honest man, and that is the most honest thing I can say of myself—that I've painted, with brush and with comforting words, pretty pictures that have done little more than distract from a more painful truth.

It was in those few dark hours of the night, around 1 am, that I was awakened by an unearthly shriek that froze my blood and set my heart pounding against my chest. A loud thumping followed interspersed with earsplitting cries of panic. I threw off my blankets and ran down the stairs to find Erik on the floor by his bed writhing in fear, drenched in sweat, and swinging his arms wildly before him in what appeared to be a night terror. I turned on the light and tried to wake him. Some seconds that felt like small eternities passed before I saw the glaze of sleep lift from his eyes, being replaced finally by recognition, followed by shock and shame.

"It was horrible!"

"It was just a dream. Everything is fine."

"I've never seen anything . . . it was so . . . "

"It's okay now. It's over. Everything's going to be all right. Let's just get you up off the floor. There we go."

"How did I end up . . . ?"

"You must have fallen out of bed."

"Did I wake you?"

"You were screaming."

"Was I? Well, it was horrible! My heart is . . . "

"It's okay, take some slow breaths." Erik sat in his bed, shaking violently, trying to breathe. He stared ahead with a mad expression that frightened me.

"They were coming for me. They came out of the darkness, and they were real."

"It wasn't real."

"What did they want with me? Why do they want me dead?"

"No one wants you dead, Erik. You had a bad dream."

"It was so real . . . " His voice shook with his body.

"You've got to cut back on the booze before bedtime. It's no wonder."

"You're right. Of course you are. I'm sorry. I'm so, so sorry I woke you up. I'm so embarrassed . . . I feel utterly insane."

"You're not insane. You just need to start taking better care of yourself, that's all."

"You're right, but . . . wait, where are you going?"

"Back to bed."

"But . . . no! You can't do that, what if they . . . what if it happens again? I can't take it again! It'll kill me this time! That darkness!"

"Leave the light on. The sun will be up soon, anyway."

"Stay with me until then . . . just until the sun comes back." I glanced up and noticed Freja peering in at the crack in the door.

"Do you want me to go get Freja?" I met her glance, hoping that she would come in and sit with Erik, but she slipped quietly out of view.

"No, no! Don't bother Freja. I don't want her to see me like this anyway. She's seen too much already. You're such a good friend. But, no! Don't leave me alone! Don't . . . oh thank you! Thank you, Elias! You're such a good person—a saint! A living saint! I don't know what I would do without you."

I did stay with him. I sat in his armchair, and watched him struggle—struggle to forget, struggle to calm his fears, struggle not to sip a little courage from the bottle on his bedside table. The strong man I had known of old lay huddled, trembling in his bed like a frightened child while I continued to assure him that everything would be okay. I am clearly not an honest man, but at that moment, I couldn't resist dwelling on Erik's words and savoring them: A living saint! Lord have mercy!

4

Last-Ditch Efforts

ALTHOUGH ERIK WAS GRATEFUL for my help while he was receiving it, his ego waxed with the morning sun. He had confronted versions of himself that threatened to topple his carefully constructed self-image—his strength and virility, his self-sufficiency, and intellectual agility. Helping him didn't bring us closer as friends. Instead, a chill resentment met me in the morning light, as though I had robbed him of something precious. He didn't want me near him and couldn't bear to have me look at him. I let him be but set up my easel on the deck instead of going into the woods, thinking that I might be needed later.

He avoided me much of the morning, and Freja, as usual, didn't come out at all. She knew better than to let him know she'd seen him at his worst. Her absence began to make more sense to me. I had thought she was simply disengaged, indifferent to his suffering. Could she be protecting his ego by refusing to see too much? She knew, of course she knew how bad things were, but she let him think she didn't if only to lessen his shame.

With the passage of a little time, Erik had reconstructed his image sufficiently, at least in his own mind, to come and sit with me on the deck. I watched with shameful amusement as he attempted to reconstruct his image in my mind as well.

"You know, Elias, there's a fine line between genius and insanity. You should know; you studied the great painters."

"Who do you mean?"

"You know, the one who cut off his ear."

"Van Gogh?"

"That's the one. It doesn't bear imagining what his paintings might have been like without that touch of the crazies." I didn't say anything but smiled and kept on painting. "Yes, this is an excellent sign. I take it as evidence of greatness to come. My biographers will talk about how my Viking lineage made me as a man, but my tortured mind truly made me as a poet."

"Your mind is tortured?"

"Oh, of course, but only in the best and most poetical of ways, you know."

"You should use it then. Write something good. Your mind is obviously ripe for it now."

"I should. I should." He didn't move but gazed out at the clouds reflected on the lake, and I continued to paint. "Look at you!" He finally exclaimed. "You're so productive! How many paintings have you done since you came?"

"Six."

"I can't believe how productive you are! And I haven't seen you take a drink since you arrived. Are you taking something special? You're not doing some sort of herbal something or other?"

"Herbal? No. I don't drink anymore, though."

"What, nothing?"

"No, I haven't had a drink in months."

"Well, I'll be damned. You know what I'm going to do? I'm going to lay off the booze too and see how productive I can be! I'll do it! This is my last drink, right here, this one—watch me drink it . . . are you watching?"

"I'm watching."

"The last drink you'll see me take while you're here. From now on, I'm teetotal! I'm reformed! I'm going to be a productive writer this summer. Reclaim my path to literary immortality. You'll see!" He took a final gulp from his whiskey glass and slammed it down on the deck railing with finality. "A new era, my friend! New poems. A new me! This is just the beginning!"

"You sure you don't want to cut back more slowly . . . gradually?"

"Slowly? Gradually? Why? You think I'm weak? I can stop whenever I want!"

"Not weak. No one said weak. But your body is used to . . . "

"My body does whatever the hell I tell it to do. It's my *mind* with the endearing, highly literary brand of madness!"

"Still, you don't want to make yourself . . . "

"It's fine, Elias! It's fine. You should be happy. I'm taking a leaf from your book. Now take a leaf from mine and try some low-level insanity. It might do wonders for your art." Having, in his mind, reasserted his superiority as the great man of letters handing down sage advice to his pupil, he returned to his room to fetch his notebook and favorite pen.

In his mind, Erik was convinced he needed sobriety. His body, however, had become accustomed to his chronic heavy drinking over the years, and I worried about the abruptness of this new resolution and how it might affect him physically, considering how fragile he had become. He wouldn't hear caution, however, and would not accept the suggestion that his body might respond unpleasantly, believing himself to be still very robust. I watched him closely over the next few days.

It started with tremors of the small musculatures of the fingers, then of his lips and eyelids. His already disturbed sleep worsened with an anxious restlessness. He was low. Too low to write. Too low to talk. I worried for him but hoped this would prove to be the worst of his withdrawal.

One warm early afternoon, I came into the cottage sooner than usual from a hike through the woods with my easel. This was usually the time of day when Erik slept, but as I entered, I didn't see his familiar sleeping form in his armchair. I thought maybe he had grasped some inspiration finally and gone to his room to write. I crept quietly down the hallway toward his room, thinking I might find him hard at work, writing at his massive mahogany desk. I heard a rustling sound and a muffled voice within. I tapped quietly, then opened the door. Erik was not at his desk, nor in his bed. The sounds came from underneath the desk.

"Erik! What are you doing?" I grabbed at him, trying to wrestle him out from under his desk, where he sat huddled, gouging and clawing frantically at his own bloodied face and arms with his fingernails—a scene I felt I'd seen before in the smokescreen of an evening pipe.

"Get them off of me! Help me! They're everywhere!"

"What? What are you talking about!"

"Look! Look! Thousands of them! All over me! Crawling everywhere, biting me!"

"There's nothing! There's nothing there! You're hurting yourself!"

"I can't get them off! Help me! Don't just stand there staring!"

"Stop doing that! Come out of there!"

"More are coming! They're coming! So many more! They're hurting me! Make them stop! Why are you just standing there?"

"Erik, nothing is hurting you . . . you're hurting yourself! There's nothing here! It's DTs! It's got to be! It's not real! Listen to me!"

"Do something! Get them off of me! Get them off!"

"I don't know what to do! God help me . . . I don't know what to do!"

I pulled him out from under the desk and wrestled him into his bed. He shrieked madly, pointing to the walls, which were crawling with armies of advancing spiders. He tried still to tear the skin on his arms and face, which he had already badly shredded with his nails. I wrapped him tightly in his blanket and sat on him to prevent him from inflicting further damage to himself. I stayed with him as he yelled profanities and screamed terribly until he seemed to pass out of consciousness. Startled, I felt for a pulse. It was rapid but seemed strong. I stayed with him until nightfall. I sat with him through the night—through the horrors—through the snakes and beetles and fantastical creatures. He quieted, and I dozed off. Early morning sunshine woke me to the stale smells of spirits which he had found in his bedside table during the night while I was asleep. He was ill in his bed for some days following, a bottle by the lamp, and a reeking wastebasket by the bed.

5

The Vanishing Point of Reason

MORNINGS WERE PARTICULARLY DISMAL for Erik, especially after his experiment with abrupt sobriety and the apparent delirium tremens that resulted. He feared the new day, perhaps because it never brought him any good, but only an aching sense of non-existence. He rose late, feeling lousy and ashamed. He would brew himself a strong pot of coffee, to which he added a generous splash of single malt whiskey. "Hair of the dog," he would say. When he remembered his night disturbances, which were becoming more frequent and dramatic, he always apologized, shaking his head in disbelief. "I'm not bonkers; I don't know what happened. Just a one-off, I guess. The price you pay for creativity and imagination. Still, I think I'll go lighter on the spirits today. No cold turkey like last time, though." Yet, any resolution to cut back never made it past noon.

In the midday sun, he seemed to warm a little and come back to life for a time, occasionally feeling motivated to take out his canoe and go fishing. But the silence of the lake, the quiet act of fishing, only amplified the overwhelming mental ruckus. By the time he returned, fishless, it was clear that the drink, his opiate, and brief comfort, had already possessed him, gripping him inwardly in its cloying embrace. It clung to him desperately and passionately, influencing every unstable thought and every teetering action. His cheeks burned red with the headiness of his liquid love, which, far from loving him back, left him utterly gutted and empty.

"It's not as if the booze makes it go away, you know," he told me once, "it doesn't."

"Why, then? Why do you do this to yourself?"

"The booze makes it all seem important . . . lofty. Meaningful. Without it, everything is just blackness—a wasteland of senseless pain. At least the booze can make me believe it's for something."

"And what does it tell you your pain is for?"

"It tells me it's for my glory. It's not absurd and useless. It's high and lofty . . . my privilege to feel. And why shouldn't I be allowed to feel that way? Why shouldn't my pain feel important and grand and high? Let me feel my greatness again, just a little, if only in my capacity to suffer great pain in the cause of worship! Damn it, Elias! Let me be tragic!"

"But it's not real. Maybe it is worth feeling. Maybe it is your right. But you aren't feeling it as it truly is. You're leaning into a caricature of pain, not the real thing."

"No, no . . . I can't bear the real thing. I fear it more than death!"

"But why?"

"The real thing—the real pain—is somewhere in the Void. I can't go in there. I can't . . . it's too terrible. Too great. It's too awful! It's personal, Elias! It knows me!"

"Personal? What are you talking about? The Void isn't an intelligence; it's just a concept. The concept of infinite space. It's an idea, not a person." I said. He looked at me long through bloodshot eyes.

"I hope you're right . . . I fear you're not."

Freja left her room less and less. In the previous years, dinner had been the one time when we all gathered, but as the day dragged on, Freja had begun to take more of her meals in her room, only coming out briefly when Erik was sleeping. She wouldn't allow him the opportunity to embarrass himself in front of her. It would have been easy to interpret her absence as frigidity and selfishness. Still, something told me it was her way of preserving the last remaining mists of illusion that had held their marriage together. I had taken responsibility for feeding Erik who, by evening, fell to his feed like a hog to swill. I remember one evening when I had placed a large glass of water in front of him, hoping he would attempt to rehydrate, he splashed it in my face, laughing: "water is for lakes and fishes, for coffee and for washing dishes! You've been poemed!"

If a day in Erik's sanity, from waking to sleeping, could be depicted as a road stretching toward the horizon, then it was shortly after dinner that his road reached its vanishing point. On the deck, he drank and laughed and cried and hollered at that midsummer sun that refused to set and free him from its blinding light. "Stop sun! Stop it! Stop it! Go away!" He would hurl empty bottles at its face, which splashed into the lake, sinking into its black depths.

"Look, I know you're unhappy. I know things haven't gone the way you'd hoped, but this drinking to forget is killing you!"

"I told you! I'm not forgetting! It's my pain—my glorious, glorious pain! Let me feel it! Let me remember it as I wish to and let me deal with it my own way!"

I believe he knew somehow, that this pain was his sacrifice, finally coming up due. I had never realized because it goes against reason. I had never realized because I had never consciously felt his kind of disappointed worship and its companion of bitter despair. I could not comprehend the unlikely truth, that it could be more difficult for a man to deny himself pain than pleasure. That self-indulgence may take its consummate form not in feasting on life's pleasures but in allowing one's self the exquisite pain of wallowing and drowning in its gall for the glory of it. Erik's indulgence in suffering, while ever struggling free of the reality that gave him such pain, imprisoned him through a paradoxical bondage to the means of his perceived freedom. Each struggle to free his tortured mind only served to tighten his bonds. That was his choice.

Did a part of me take pleasure in his troubles? Find a modicum of secret enjoyment with each fresh incident that drove this drama further into the madness from which there was increasingly little hope of return? Did it give me a secret thrill to see him slip from his lofty mountain, falling farther every day, and flailing about, drowning in the cold sea of mortality like myself? If it did, I never admitted it to myself. I only ever kept a calculated record of my sympathy, worry, and hope for his recovery in my journal, which I had started keeping during my first summer with him as evidence of my good intentions. And that too was true. It was not a question of feeling one way or the other but of feeling all of these things battling within me while acknowledging only the thoughts that bolstered my own feelings of growing superiority. Seeing my kind, compassionate words in writing somehow made them irrefutable.

Perhaps it is these half-truths we tell ourselves which are, in the end, the most damning. I told the invisible examiner of my journal that I wanted Erik to be better. I told myself that I wanted the two of them to be reconciled and happy again. Telling myself these isolated hopes kept me deeply entrenched in a business that didn't concern me, where full self-honesty might have encouraged appropriate distance. Telling myself this half-truth justified my involvement to myself, an involvement that I wish I could erase forever from my personal history.

As the summer progressed, Erik continued to teeter between irrational and sometimes paranoid states with only short bursts of calm, clear thought usually occurring in the late morning. By afternoon, his behavior was more unpredictable. I remember one late afternoon as I came from the woods with my sketchpad, I noticed Erik staring at me from his armchair by the window. He appeared calm and even deep in thought.

"What's up?" I finally asked, kicking off my shoes and sitting next to him. He looked at me through narrowed eyes.

"Do you know what's always bothered me, Elias?"

"Besides literary critics, you mean?"

"Your accent."

"What do you mean?" I asked, a little offended.

"You haven't got one."

"Thanks!"

"And your words . . . " he continued.

"Which ones?"

"How is it that you know such complicated words, like illusion, dimension, perspective . . . conscription. So many polysyllabic Latinate words in your repertoire. Too many."

"I'm not sure what you're asking me . . . " I said. He sat forward, his eyes widening, staring unwaveringly at my own.

"You say you grew up speaking Russian and Polish, but you sound like a native New Yorker. You have all these sad stories of life as a child in the Middle East—"

"Eastern Europe."

"—and there's nothing foreign about you at all . . . nothing at all."

" . . . well . . . "

"Who the hell are you, and why are you pretending to be my friend?" he demanded.

"What?"

"Nothing adds up! Your stories don't check out. The only thing I can figure is that you're a spook!"

"A spook?"

"A spy, a spy! Oh treachery! You say things about our army men doing bad things in Vietnam, you toast in Russian, you write secrets in your little book, and you're always hanging around trying to make me talk! Every day you try to make me talk! Who the hell are you, and what do you want from me?" His face was red, and a vein was beginning to stand up on his forehead.

"Erik, I'm—"

"Papers!"

"What?"

"Come on! Now! I want to see your papers!"

"What papers?"

"Passport. Visa. Birth certificate."

"Erik, I'm an American citizen. I don't even have a passport, and I don't need a visa anymore. I might have had a birth certificate at one time, but I have no idea what became of it. I have a driver's license; would you like to see it?"

"Fork it over!" I pulled the little-used card from my wallet and handed it to him. He appeared to scrutinize it, looking up at me suspiciously every few seconds, as though I might pull a handgun or cyanide pill from my shoe at any moment.

"You may not be political . . . "

"No. Absolutely not."

"But how do I know you aren't here to raid my notebooks and steal my ideas for yourself! You're good with words. Too good. I don't know why it never occurred to me before that you might be looking to make off with my poems before they're safely published!"

"What poems? You hardly ever write a word." I was becoming annoyed.

"No, you *are* a spy! You want to know if I've been evading my taxes and hiding money away," he said, trying another angle. "It's *my* money! It's *my* inheritance!"

"Erik, for crying out loud, I'm your friend! We've known each other since freshman year at Columbia. I know big words because I went to college and I read books. I don't have an accent (at least not a Polish one) because I learned English very young and worked hard in school. My mother made sure of that. Accents are bullied, and I worked especially hard to stop getting beaten up for the way I talked . . . but that's something you wouldn't understand, would you? You were probably one of the kids doing the bullying back then. You've never been on the outside of any group. And yes, I do have questions about Vietnam, why our military was there in the first place. I do, because of the men I've met who came back and told me things—broken men living in boxes on the street. I have no conclusions, no political agenda, just questions! And I try to talk to you every day because you're my friend! It's rude to stay in someone's house without ever talking to them, don't you think?" I tried to keep my tone even and calm, but my frustration was evident. I could see him settling back into his armchair, considering my words.

"Oh, I suppose, I suppose, I suppose." He said at last. "I was just joking you; don't you know? I wasn't serious. You didn't think I meant all that!" He tossed back my driver's license, which fell several feet to the right of its target.

"You sounded pretty serious to me."

"Well, I wasn't. I was just joking."

"Seriously paranoid . . . " I ventured.

"It was a joke, Elias! Get a sense of humor!" he finally boomed. "Laugh, damn you!" He was silent and shifting uneasily in his chair, peering at me from the corner of his eye. "I'm going for a walk," he finally said and rushed unsteadily out into the garden.

" . . . okay," I said more to myself than to him and watched him stumble through the unkempt garden rows, stepping haphazardly on the half-formed fruits.

While more and more of my time with Erik reflected the poison of dark thoughts and paranoid suspicions, there were moments in the late morning, precious and brief, when his thoughts came into sharper focus. It was in these moments that he was gripped with a sense of urgency to explain to me, to spare me perhaps, from something he was beginning to understand, but labored to put into words. He tried to make me understand, as well. Something had dawned upon him during his descent. Some profound truth which he had only pretended to possess in health, had finally been glimpsed in his escalating madness.

In one of those moments, he grabbed me, roughly, emphatically, pulling me into a deck chair next to him. His breath reeked, and his eyes fixed on me unwaveringly as he spoke, slowly, but with great importance.

"Elias, tell me. What is a human being's most essential action?"

"Essential action?"

"Yes. What act is most essential to human existence?"

"Easy. Eating. Drinking. Sleeping. Using the toilet . . . "

"What? No! Don't be simple! Every creature, every amoeba, does all that! I mean, what essential action makes us truly human? What do we do, what must we do, that sets us apart from other creatures and defines our humanity?" His voice was insistent and disturbingly humorless.

"Well, why didn't you say you wanted to talk metaphysics? Beauty. That's our essential action. We love beauty and make things that have no practical use except to be beautiful. We are artistic creatures. We are creative. We must create beautiful things, or else we are not acting out of the fullness of our humanity." I offered what I thought then was a decent answer, but he looked disappointed, almost offended.

"Presumptuous poppycock," he muttered.

"Excuse me?"

"You mean to say you don't think animals appreciate beauty? And here I thought you were some sort of advocate for the non-human creatures. How can you possibly know that they don't appreciate beauty? When the weaver bird takes such pains to build its cathedral nests, or when the female birds of paradise in New Guinea choose only the most ornately plumed mates with the most beautiful songs and dances? It's a nice thought. Very romantic. I'm sure as an artist, it's a great temptation to put your craft at the center of every truly human action, but it's a lie."

"What then?" I asked, becoming annoyed as I felt the status quo threatening to return—my intellectual inferiority to him. "You obviously thought you knew the answer before you asked me, so let's have it."

"I do know the answer now. I used to think more along those lines, like you. I thought that poetry and art, the creative faculty were the essential functions of humanity. And if not the creative faculty, then at least the intellectual faculty. Reason. But that's all puffed up thinking, don't you see? Animals are creative and intelligent in their own ways, but did you ever think that they are miles ahead of us?"

"How so?"

"They need so little. Their essential actions are so simple and pure. Our essential action betrays our defect—a defect that they don't share." He said this impressively, and I started losing patience with him, though I believe I hid it well enough.

"And what defect is that?"

"We, my friend, are hungering souls."

"Hungering souls?"

"Yes. Hungering souls. Discovering and rediscovering our own emptiness, generation after generation, the Void in all its infinitude hiding in plain view at the core of our being."

"You're going to talk about the Void again? We've been there. Are we still there?"

"Of course we're still there. We never left it, because it never left us! We're all so inwardly spacious . . . so very, very spacious for such tiny creatures in this vast universe. So very spacious, and so very hungry. But the more we try to feed that hunger, to fill that inner void, the hungrier we become. You know! You must know! You remember Gertrude? She loved the king so much, 'as if increase of appetite had grown by what it fed on! And yet within a month!' Hamlet! He was halfway there! But no! Frailty, thy name is *human*! We consume each other with such voracious abandon, then completely lose interest because it's never enough! We utterly deplete each other. Do you hear me? It is never enough! We're always left so painfully empty—left hungrier by all we devour along the way. It's all suffering and emptiness . . . the dark. You *do* know, don't you? If you don't, you will."

"I know the Void well enough. But you said essential *action* not essential characteristic." I liked saying that. There is superiority in stressing semantics.

"I did mean action. Wait for it: so, if the vastness of our emptiness defines our humanity, then our most essential action, as humans, is filling our emptiness. This is an emptiness that animals don't possess. They're complete—whole—their only concern is us when our defect affects them."

"I'm not sure I—"

"We are *homo adorans*! Of course, we *think* things, and we *make* things, but we are truly the creature who must *worship*! That is our essential action! Our purpose! Don't you see? We can't live without worship! Maybe the word hits you wrong. You can protest all you like, but one day you'll realize that it's true . . . someday when it's too late, and you realize that all this time you've been worshipping a pretty particle of pollen, on a flower too big to be seen. We're all quite small, you know. We imagine ourselves to be titans, gods. But we're tiny, frail shells, much tinier in fact than the emptiness we conceal. We all expand inwardly—boundlessly. That's what makes us human. That's what scares me. It should scare you too, but you've got too much clutter and too many demigods taking up space to take notice. It hasn't come crashing down on you yet. But they'll fail you! They will all fail you, and you will fail yourself!" He was becoming increasingly animated, and his face was turning an ugly purple.

"Maybe you should go take a rest . . . "

"I've offended you. I don't mean to offend you. Really. I'm warning you. You reach a certain point where you can't turn back . . . you've gone too far and sacrificed too much. The time comes when you have to reap the harvest of your thoughts and loves and worship. I'm reaping them now. And let me tell you, it's a bitter crop."

I listened to him, but I didn't hear him. I wasn't able. I didn't understand his words then. I only smiled to myself inwardly, thinking how absurd he had become, and how he had caused himself to deteriorate. How he still pretended at deeply philosophical talk while only nonsense came out—nonsense and bad breath! How I thought that I pitied him! I nodded and appeased him in condescension, and in the dark places of my mind, benignly calculated his demise.

6

How to Paint the Portrait of a Goddess

Or Pretentious Reflections on the Artistic Process

HOW DO YOU PAINT the portrait of a goddess? I questioned at several points
why I had offered such a service considering the many ways that I could
fail. Still, I convinced myself that it was a mission to help my friend rediscover the sufficiency of the life he had, and eventually restore his health.
That, of course, was idealistic, but I thought if nothing else, it might make
him feel a little better temporarily without alcohol. Like all propaganda, it
would succeed if only because he wanted it to succeed. I was a good friend.
I was helping. I was also eager for the opportunity to prove my original
thesis—that truth is preferable to fact, and thus that painting is superior
to photography. The struggle was in discovering what the truth I meant to
capture with this portrait actually was. Where was I to find it, and having
found it, how was I to translate it?

I revisited the infamous black and white photos from that first summer, scrutinizing them for the truth (if indeed there was any) that my
young friend had dared to present in the same subject. It had been a while
since I'd looked at those pictures, but I felt that if I was going to create a
portrait of Erik's goddess that would prove a tonic to his distemper, I would
have to finally understand the pictures that had caused such anger in both
him and Freja.

I spread the prints out on my bed and examined them once again. Time, distance, and experience do help in understanding a work of art at last, and the first thing that struck me in this new evaluation was that she had taken some liberties with the physical laws which would typically determine the lights and shadows of the scene. My friend had created a visual language through value, which I could only interpret as gloom, menace, and foreboding. How much of this mood was her doing? Tricks of the trade adeptly applied in the darkroom or the settings of her camera? How much of what I was seeing was the actual revelation of gathering darkness—or a darkness already fully present about the subject—hidden in the lively colors now stripped away so cruelly?

It was no wonder she chose to work with achromatic values, eschewing the popular color film, which had been Erik's particular request that summer. Just as some paintings, if photographed in black and white, will expose the artist's disregard (or ignorance?) of the actual value relationships of some colors, Freja photographed in black and white, was exposed in the same error. While she sparkled in full color, in black and white, all of those carefully applied colors became of equal value, showing a face of flat gray with only deeper tones about the eyes and the hollows of her cheeks. This miscalculation of chromatic values on her part revealed a sickly, skeletal appearance. While her color palette could stun and stupefy in the golden light of the midsummer garden, her desaturated canvas revealed some of the pain and fear (and perhaps hidden years?) which had been masked by the springtime hues applied in the privacy of her studio. All of this, with the employment of chiaroscuro, enveloped darkness and menacing space, served as a cruel exposé of all that Freja had labored to create.

I began to understand that those pictures did show a greater truth about Freja, and only after knowing Freja better, being allowed into her studio and hearing her fears and insecurities, did I believe the shadows. I believed them because I had been allowed to see what others hadn't—her vulnerability and her humanity. Now I could draw her—now that she was human to me and no longer a goddess. But this was a truth which couldn't be told, at least if my painting was going to serve the propagandistic function I intended. One thing was certain. If I was going to paint the portrait of a goddess, it must be in full, vibrant color. I must obscure the contrasts of light and darkness. I must use my colors to ease the truth, to lift the shadows, and reveal a golden goddess who, perhaps, never was. I must tell Erik what to see.

I've walked alone through the thick, old-growth forest and sat alone by the deep, dark lake. I've lain alone in my bed listening to the honest ring of insects throbbing throughout the night. My head is swarming and thick and full of ideas and visions and colors that chase away sleep. I sit alone in this cool early morning, my fingers gouging through the lakeshore of broken shells and smooth pebbles. A kingfisher just cut through the water's surface, plunging into the blackness as though it held no fear, no mystery, coming miraculously to the surface with a small glittering fish. A creature unafraid of the Void. I envy the kingfisher.

I am only human and think of things in human terms. If one constant of humanity is that each differs from the next, then I must ask myself how this woman is unlike others, and there I must paint her in the phenomena that set her apart. In my mind, I see her image rising from the water like Venus from the sea foam, like my first vision of her two summers ago, a beautiful woman, bare and brazen on her rock, calling on the earth and the elements to worship her beauty. But she is not one of their kind. She is something apart. Perhaps that revelation alone is movement toward the painting I must create.

Everyone has their own approach to artistic creation. While some might gather their inspiration from noise, action, and happy time spent in the company of others, my moments of insight have only ever come when I'm alone, in the quiet and fresh air. In my mind, I see myself as simultaneously a tree and a horticulturalist. For although it would be simple enough to say that my art grows from my branches as blushing fruits ready to pick, it would belie the effort required for their cultivation. No, art doesn't simply grow of its own accord; at least I have never been so lucky. I must prune back the worthless bits to encourage new growth. I must give it plenty of nourishment through long refreshing drinks from other artists' triumphs and fertilize with what is true and beautiful in other art forms. Then, as the flowers begin to unfold, I must protect them from the cold snaps of critical opinion by sheltering them in my secret garden until they can warm and ripen in the sun. It takes time and patience to grow a painting. The worst (and easiest) of sins is to pick it too soon. Then you can only lament what it could have been.

You pretentious ass. I'm ashamed of you.

Freja has conceded that I have "talent," but her words have had the opposite effect than she perhaps intended. I think one of the most hurtful things to tell an artist is that he is talented. The "talented" artist, it might be assumed, is born that way. His art is not the result of years of toil and obsessive refining of his skills, but somehow of a genetic fluke that made him more artistic than his brother. Artistic ability cannot be defined as some mere physical propensity for working with one's hands. One could as well be a dentist or a surgeon or a machinist if a steady hand and attention to detail were the only criteria. Artistic skill is the combination of obsession with forcing one's hands to learn how to create what one sees, optically or mentally, with the poetic turn of mind that sees the truth and subtler beauty beneath the surface of things. Those who complain that they don't have a talent for art are unaware that such a gift was hard-won through the toil of desperate pursuit. It is won through the frustration of repeated effort in spite of repeated failure, rather than simply discovered one day on the playground like a shiny pebble one could carry in one's pocket and trade for chewing gum.

Obsessive, yes. An obsessive and pretentious ass.

I have, through years of painstaking effort, achieved a small degree of proficiency in my art, and perhaps the most crucial evidence of that proficiency is the understanding of how to grow a painting in the particular soil of my own creative orchard. I know at least how to bring the fruit to formation, but allowing it to ripen often takes more patience, unfortunately, than I appear to possess at present. For me, paintings grow in sunshine. I stay outside now as long as the sun remains with me. I sit silently while my mind throngs with the music of ideas, which, instead of swarming in deafening discordance, is now beginning to harmonize. I stroll aimlessly in body, while my mind focuses on its destination and runs to meet it like a long-separated lover. I stare ahead without really seeing anything but the painting as it forms itself in my mind.

Humility is an endless road,
but you're not even on it.

I've seen it finally, in its fullness! Under a spruce tree, in a bed of needles, under the brittle, webbed skeleton of a dried leaf, in the echoing bugle of a far-off elk, in the dying embers of the late-setting sun. I've seen it in all clarity. It vibrates with power, potency, potential—a pretty bit of borderline propaganda that might do my suffering friend some good.

How I let myself lie.

7

The Painting

IN THE QUIET OF the old-growth forest, time seemed to stop. That microscopic line that we call the present, the insubstantial division between things past and things yet to come, expanded. The present, rather than merely a transitory state, a line to cross, or a small archway between past and future, became its own rich plane full of significance and truth. The edges of reality sharpened. Instead of a blur of motion like the landscape flying by the window of some high-speed train, the present became still, calm, and substantial. It was not a feeling of timelessness, as though time had ceased to exist, or lost its reality, but rather a sense of "timefulness." The Ancients might have called it "Kairos"—a "now" so significant and poignant, that it feels almost outside of time as we usually experience it.

Time didn't just happen to me in that woodland, by that lake. Time didn't make me its victim, another creature to be ravaged by its passing. I was absorbed into the moment and felt a oneness with it. Do I sound insane? Maybe I am. Maybe we are all insane, every terribly busy day of our terribly busy lives, save for those rare moments when we finally notice the reality, even the eternity, of the present moment. To live in the past or dream of the future is to live a non-existence, a fantasy of our making or memory. The present moment, if we could stay in it longer than a few seconds without panicking, is where we find the truth.

Idyllic as the still present may sound, or indeed seemed at first to me, it exposed my inner void in a brutal light. I felt the reality of my own existence as a mere fragile wood shaving, curling 'round its own inner emptiness, just as Erik had described it. Having tasted solitude and the "timefulness" of the present, I believe this to be true of most of us. We can speed through time, chasing some vision of the future like the man who runs to the front of the train to reach the next station faster. We rarely pause to peer inside of ourselves. For me, the emptiness was nothing compared to the horror of finding an actual presence lurking in the darkness of my hollow center. Creatures unacknowledged, monsters, cowards, thieves, and villains of the worst description. Journeys to the center of the self reveal the person more hateful to us than any tyrant of human history—our own true selves— wounded creatures, scheming creatures. I ignored them all and painted.

Woven organic fiber anointed with a paste formed of fine marble dust, clean water, and rabbit skin glue—plant, rock, water, and flesh will form the foundation of my masterpiece. The yolk of an egg—a creature of the air. A splash of vinegar—the fruit of the vine. Ground up raw minerals—an ancient and elemental medium. Egg tempera and burnished red clay, a recipe for the earthly rendering of a divine portrait.

I sketch the sacred moment from behind—arms upraised and chest to heaven. I sketch her on her rock, glancing boldly over her shoulder as if to acknowledge and sanction the viewer's presence. Just enough to guide me as I apply my layers of pigment. Her naked skin, titanium white only in foundation, is kissed with the pale and golden ochre of the sun, her features defined by shadows of azurite. In Bavarian green earth, raw sienna, terre verte, raw umber, and earth orange, the trees and plants, her cathedral dome, cast shadows of natural malachite. Caput Mortuum Dark, violet brown, defines the hardest edges of rock and water's surface. Cadmium yellows, realgar, Alizarin crimson, and hematite—the faces of flowers, the caps of mushrooms, the secret flash of feathers, the Indian yellow beaks that sing praise through olive green leaves. Pale ochre and titanium white, the soft wings of Lymantria Dispar Dispar, the gypsy moth, may ultimately take time to notice (if it's noticed at all), but I know it's there and why. My self-portrait as a moth, drawn to her light.

An invasive species, or didn't you know?

These pigments streak, reflected, on the water, and she is reflected there too in the brash detail warranted by her act. Spreading over and reaching into every corner of the scene, the sun! Layers of ochre, cadmium, and realgar, it rises in the midsummer morning, the source of all highlight and shadow.

I've scarcely left my room this summer, except in the early morning to walk in the woods, breathe, and rest my hands and eyes. Even in my sleep, I don't seem to rest, as my activity continues in my too-real dreams. I paint all through the night in my mind. I see Erik rarely. He sleeps through the day and drinks while I sleep. We see each other only at dinner, and even then, our conversation is scant. He asks what I've been doing, and I tell him I've been painting. That seems to satisfy him that I don't need entertaining, and he carries on with his habits.

The painting has been taking shape in my hands. I'm beginning to see something I've never seen before in my work. What is it? I can't name it, but it excites me beyond all expectations. It motivated me to keep painting late into the night last night, still laying one pigment over another, sculpting her form of light and shadow, or form and hollow, until finally, around 2:57 A.M., she seemed to breathe! How can I describe the moment when a picture suddenly becomes a living thing? I've done it! Is this not the goal of art? To create something real? If I have ever allowed myself to believe that I've achieved such a miracle before this point—before this picture—I blush at my ignorance.

The sun was just setting tonight when I applied the ultimate stroke, the final caress that created flesh, and atmosphere, and the faintest breath of wind through the leaves where moments earlier there had been only paint.

Starting a picture is hard enough but finishing it can be agony. The ever-dissatisfied artist can always find something that could be better. Some value that must be deepened, some feeling that could be intensified. Finishing a painting can be as painful as tearing one's own flesh, so much has it become a part of the artist's being. As I held my brush lightly in my hand tonight, poised over this living, breathing organism before me, I knew that any other mark would be sacrilege. She is finished; she is perfect. Dipping the tip of my finest brush in the glooming pool of Caput Mortuum Dark, I now make the only mark I can by gently placing my name in the lower-left corner, resting among the pebbles and shells of the lakeshore.

Lord have mercy.

It is inevitable in life, perhaps more in these times than ever before, that there will be those people in our lives who are somehow left behind, or who leave us behind. Those with whom we were close for a time, or might have been, given time to cultivate a connection beyond acquaintance. Then they vanish—like a note of music which fades away so quickly, leaving only the memory of a feeling. Perhaps we approach each other only as passersby who, by some coincidence, happen to be moving in the same direction for a time, or whose paths cross only briefly. Yet, the fact of their having shared a brief yet poignant moment with us alters our perspective forever. Their memory lives on like that note of music that enters the head unbidden one day while weeding the garden or taking a shower. Sometimes whole conversations flood back, while other times only a single word.

Perception.

That was her word. Of all moments, of all memories, that word, that dangling question is the one that returns, like a phantom, asking and re-asking me to examine the reality of my perception. But I was so young then, and so ready to believe in illusions, to give them my fealty and loyalty and love. It was difficult to heed the challenge to take a step back and widen my view of the canvas when I had fallen in love with some little isolated corner of the picture, stubbornly imposing interpretations of what amounted to be a mere pebble on the shore. But so enamored had I become of the little universe I'd invented around that little spot that the mere suggestion that I was missing the larger whole seemed offensive. I needed a hand, a real, firm, loving hand to grasp my own and lead me to a better vantage point to expose the simulacrum. How much better it must be to face that moment with another, sympathetic soul.

But she only gave me a word, not a hand. And the slow, painful process of backing away on my own revealed the truth too late and without a sympathetic hand to hold. But that is the nature of these passersby. They give us just a hint, a nudge, a word, a seed, then the rest we must face alone. But that word, that seed, may not mean a thing until the time is ripe, and until that time, it may lay dormant or misinterpreted. And at that moment, I did misinterpret, standing before my finished painting, finally taking a step back. I took in the scene as a whole, instead of microscopically finessing details. To me, the perspective looked perfect.

8

The Zoo is Closed

AT SOME POINT, THE question had to be posed, although it didn't feel like mine to ask. It hung like a silent specter over every day now, seeming one moment like a possible solution and a tonic for the man deteriorating in seclusion on his porch, bottle in hand, while the next moment seeming laughably absurd. Was there to be a midsummer garden party this year or not? Erik had always taken such pride and pleasure in the planning, in the food and the maypole and Freja's new summer dresses, so photogenic in the sun-dappled garden.

Erik was not in a position to muster the motivation necessary to plan and execute such an event. Freja's increasing secrecy and passivity kept her from making an effort to plan any entertainment of that kind, especially considering the distinct possibility of Erik's current condition causing everyone embarrassment. I wondered, though, if the opportunity to get into some lively, boisterous company and see Freja floating around the garden again looking absolutely in possession of every eye might do Erik some good.

"Have you given much thought to midsummer this year?" I asked casually as Erik gulped down his coffee one morning.

"What about it?" he growled.

"You know . . . how we'll celebrate."

"Celebrate what? The fertility of the earth and the animals and some people?"

"The long days, the strawberries, the pickled herrings, and naughty songs . . . your noble Viking roots . . . "

"The booze . . . "

"The company?"

"I don't require company for that."

"It's better with friends."

"What friends?"

"Well, I don't know. Don't you always have some friends come to celebrate with you? I thought it was a tradition."

"Gawkers."

"What?"

"You heard me. They came to see a great poet with his beautiful goddess living a charmed existence—an enviable existence. That's what we played at because that's what they said we were, and that's what we were always supposed to be. You become whatever they say you are, you know, or you at least pretend. And the more you play at it, the more all the expectations will crush you when the mask finally slips. Now they would come to gawk at the drunken madman who hasn't written a decent verse in years and whose wife, quite mysteriously, never seems to age. Why, she must get her face lifted, and put an extraordinary amount of effort into ensuring that when her madman finally offs himself, she'll have the face to enslave her next worshipper. Do they pity me? Ha! They just want to watch the whole farcical performance and thank the aerial spirits that they aren't me!"

"Don't you think you're being a tad paranoid?"

"The zoo is closed, Elias! Drop it!"

I did let the matter drop. Perhaps it would be enough to feed him some strawberries and present him with the painting on our own for midsummer. Maybe I could groom him sufficiently that Freja would even come out and join us in the garden for a little while. But at that moment, all I could do was sit by him in silence as he stared desperately into his coffee cup.

"I can't go on like this. There's just no point," he said at last.

"Well, does there have to be a point?"

"Damn it, Elias! Of course there has to be a point! A man can survive inhuman tortures, deprivation, humiliation, starvation, but he cannot survive without a point, no matter how safe and well-fed his body is. No amount of physical comfort or psychoanalysis can make up for the lack of it."

"And yours was Freja?"

"She was my everything, and where is she now? I don't know what's worse . . . her seeing what I've become or refusing to see it. You can't possibly understand, Elias. She was just . . . everything."

"Well, is that fair?"

"Fair? It's not as though she wanted anything less. We wrote this epic together. But she couldn't go the distance, could she?"

"Go the distance? She's still here, isn't she? She could have left you. It's not as though you've made yourself particularly lovable lately. Anyway, she's only human." He held his head between his hands as if to contain an explosion, rocking back and forth in his chair.

"I can't go on," he kept repeating, "I can't go on." He shook violently, feverishly, straining to regain control. "You're right," he finally said, through trembling lips. "She *is* still here. It's me. I'm a coward. I'm nothing but a stinking, milk-livered coward."

"Don't say that."

"It's true. It's the only truth in this whole rat's nest of lies and illusions. I'll live. She'll stay. I'll suffer and go mad, but I'll live, and she'll stay."

"That doesn't sound so cowardly to me."

"Because you're not comprehending. I'm the one who holds the pen. The ultimate option is always within reach. I can end the story! It has to end eventually. Did you think this could go on forever? I can end the story, and with it, my suffering . . . I just haven't got the guts to do it."

On Midsummer's Eve, I wrote this in my journal as I lay in my bed, the late dusky light shining blue through the curtain lace. I read it now, and it still terrifies me, perhaps even more now than it did then:

I'm beginning to distrust Time. I'm not sure it actually exists, at least not as I've imagined it. It has always seemed like a force—a rapid current—something inevitable that just keeps flowing, dragging us ever onward. To what? To the end, dung and death like all other living creatures? But what if Time is just a way of looking at the world . . . a way of organizing it so that it doesn't bend (or break) our minds to contemplate the possibility that all Time—past, present, and future—is Now if we pause long enough to see them all converge. But it's hard to see. It's hard to stay long enough in that state of quiet watchfulness and really see it.

I don't know. I'm afraid I might be losing my mind. But I think I just felt time stop as I was lying in bed this evening. It happened in an instant, to employ a word that used to make sense to me. I was just lying here, noticing the quiet, noticing the pattern of the paint on the ceiling. Noticing the shapes in it like with clouds—the howling wolf, the hippo, the ghost—I didn't even shut my eyes, but it felt as though my mind blinked. It was like when the power flickers briefly, and you doubt yourself for a moment until someone else confirms it. Was it my mind, or some other organ I didn't know I possessed? It blinked and opened, some inner vision that pierced the thin façade of the room around me, past the shapes in the ceiling paint, past the walls and the curtains and the woods and darkening sky beyond them. Everything fell away, and there was a crowd of people, all watching me. At the forefront of the crowd, I saw a little boy holding a basket of mushrooms. He stood there crying, clinging to an old man's hand—a man I didn't know, but his eyes looked so much like my grandmother's. Why did they all look at me? Why with such sorrow? What did they know that I don't? What warning did they bring, wordlessly outside of Time? I blinked my eyes, that's all, and they were gone. The façade reasserted itself—the trees, the walls, the ceiling, the curtain lace, fluttering before the fading blue light of the open window in a breath of wind that brought with it smells of pine and fog.

I got up out of bed and walked the perimeter of the room, feeling a little crazy as I tapped the walls lightly to confirm their reality. I no longer know how to differentiate between the actual and the fanciful. How many times have I confused them in my life? Maybe I've had everything backward. Tonight, I came so sharply, so intensely into the present moment . . . I seemed unconsciously to summon or gather a legion of my fragmented selves from the millions of moments in which I have existed in the past and have yet to exist in the future. I was completely present in one place in Time in a way I could never have imagined possible, but why did they all look at me, this one little fragment living in this one particular moment, and weep?

Perhaps the seams of my consciousness need caulking, to keep my selves from leaking through into the present again. At first, I was excited by it, but I don't think I would like it to happen again. Maybe I just need sleep. Tomorrow is an important day. I'm giving Erik his present tomorrow as soon as I've gotten the frame from town in the morning.

All will be well again. I'm sure of it.

9

The Inevitable

EARLY MIDSUMMER MORNING, I went into town to pick up the frame I'd ordered for the occasion of presenting Erik with his painting of Freja. The cottage was quiet when I left, with its inhabitants still sleeping away the golden hours of morning. I attempted to steal away without waking anyone and return before I was missed. Whether my departure was noticed, I'll never know, but at some point during my absence, the sleepers awoke—or at least one did.

While this account of what happened that morning is mostly my own evidence-based inference, I envision Erik tromping up the stairs with his heavy gait and tapping on my door. When I failed to answer, he tried the handle and, finding it unlocked, perhaps he opened it and looked in. The average day would have found me long awake already, coffee in hand. Perhaps that's why he sought me in my room, but instead of seeing me, he saw a new painting still on its easel. Something about it intrigued him, and he entered to take a closer look.

My shameless ego likes to think he admired the virtuosity of the brushstrokes and the clear earthy tones, but it was the figure in the picture that arrested his attention. There could be no doubt of its identity. He had idolized and worshipped that form, and in that moment, the instability of his accelerating paranoia combined critically with his naturally jealous nature. He erupted in an uncontrollable rage over something that, to him, was blatantly obvious. The fragile fabric of Erik's consensual hallucination with his wife was finally torn asunder, and the enchantment that had bound the two of them together in worship, however tenuously, finally dissolved.

Oh Treachery! He seethed and tore at his thinning hair with rough, trembling hands. Hadn't he been a good host? Hadn't he given me free reign of his own home with everything I needed and more? And how had I repaid him? And her! He had adored her, worshipped her, always (so he thought) put her desires before his own, and never succumbed to the crude vileness of forcing his company on her when she preferred solitude. She had betrayed him. Why had he not seen it before? She kept her own room so that she could have a lover! She hadn't wanted to have a child with him because all along she'd had someone else in mind. It was all so clear to him what had happened and how he'd turned a blind eye to an illicit relationship that he had enabled by inviting the partner of her guilt, year after year, to enter their sacred space as a trusted companion for him.

He stormed into Freja's room and presented his evidence in the broken, ireful tones of a man teetering on the edge of insanity. Perhaps she attempted to set the record straight. Perhaps she tried to calm and reassure him. But perhaps she only stared into his eyes with her grey, penetrating gaze and laughed. For some reason, that's how I envision the scene. I hear it as a cold and humorless laugh as alien and unlikely as the one I had heard once before. She laughed, of course, at the absurdity of such an accusation, but Erik heard nothing but confirmation and mockery in her reaction. He took her shoulders roughly in his large hands, bellowing incoherently in her face with poisonous breath. Still, she laughed. He dragged her, still in her thin, white nightgown, to her familiar rock by the lake, the scene of the treacherous portrait, and still, she laughed, perhaps now out of fear. His face burned and contorted with rage, and still, she laughed. She didn't stop laughing until the black water of the lake filled her lungs and, like some thin, dingy rag, she floated lifeless in the murky shallows.

He turned his tormented back on this scene of his own making and stormed back to the cottage. There was still more to be done. Now he had to confront the lover—the user—the friend turned fiend in whom he had confided and misguidedly placed his trust. He went back into my room to await my return. Perhaps he sat on the bed and looked again at the picture, that brazen, mocking, breathing picture! He took a letter opener from the desk and plunged it into the quivering heart of the canvas. The threads popped and ripped like living sinew as he tore through the scene of his naked wife's betrayal. Satisfied with the degree of disfigurement, and fatigued by the effort, he lay on the bed and waited, planning a similar fate for the artist.

But time moves slowly when a broken mind awaits such a dark and bitter task. In his impatience, he rummaged through the nightstand and found my journal. His mind flooded with the horrible anticipation of finding detailed encounters and confessions, efficiently recorded for my own future amusement. He couldn't bear the details, but neither could he resist knowing them. He opened the book and read, but instead of records of sordid encounters, he found only the pretentious artistic musings of a man who thought himself quite wise and philosophical, interspersed with the carefully, meticulously recorded worries of an all-round good egg, who had hatched a plan to help rehabilitate an ailing, heartsick friend. The plan, though feeble and naïve, was to give his friend what he claimed to be a timeless portrait of his goddess in her chapel.

The dead silence of my room was split suddenly by laughter—this time, Erik's. It was the terrible, mad, tear-jerked laughter of a man who can't cope and has ceased to try. He tossed the journal onto the floor where I would later find it, and descended the stairs, still seized with convulsions of laughter. Locking himself in his room, he took every midsummer photograph of his wife, every commissioned image of his dead goddess, and lay with them on his bed. In my mind, I see him kissing each one gently, reverently, in veneration of the one he had martyred by mistake, then reaching out toward his nightstand with a practiced gesture and shaking hand. Taking all his hoarded bottles, he drank them down like water until the darkness of that voracious void closed in upon him, and he fell asleep, clutching the photos, never conscious of that decisive moment when his weak and broken heart stopped beating.

10

Caput Mortuum

WHEN I RETURNED TO the cottage later that morning, happy and full of good coffee, bearing my custom-made frame, something white and billowy in the shallows by the lakeshore caught my eye. I walked in the sweet stupor of the sunny morning over the grass to the smooth pebbles and broken shells that traced the water's edge. I can remember how the sun, only a moment before shedding sweet, benign rays, suddenly cast a harsh and brutal light on the cold white marble face of the dead woman. Was it really Freja? It seemed like some absurd but not unfamiliar dream. In life, she had been a goddess, but in death, she was perfectly ordinary, not divine, or even remarkably beautiful. Just a poor, drowned soul still in her nightgown. Another broken shell washed to shore by the certainty of the tide—Caput Mortuum—worthless remains. Perhaps, after all, what she had been in life was just a tiny, frail, and shapeless creature hiding inside the irised convolutions of a beautiful shell, but imagination and advantageous lighting had made her sacred. Perhaps the spellbound praise of men dazzled by tricks of golden midsummer sunlight had convinced her of the lie as well, or at least of its usefulness, and even its necessity.

I don't know what appalled me more, the mortal scene uncoiled before me on the lakeshore, or the numb lack of astonishment I felt in looking at it. I was observing something that deep down in some dark, secret corner of my mind I had expected as if it were an event that somehow had to take place. I didn't need to go looking for him to know that Erik, too, was dead by his own hand. It was the way it must be—the end of their tragic poem. But why? And if I had known all along where the story was going, toward what deadly climax it was careening, why did I continue to play along, even fueling its course? I must have had a choice—several, no doubt, and I made them in the deluded confidence that I loved . . . no, not loved . . . worshipped my friends and wanted to see them reclaim their glory. But at some critical moment, one I had never allowed myself to acknowledge fully, my own worship had died, and some new animal had taken up residence in its place.

By all outward appearances, my actions had been honorable, if a little simple-minded, but the real naïveté was in allowing myself to believe my own façade. In truth, I hated them. I hated them both for their failure, for their fall, for their frailty. Freja had been right all along, at least in part. When worship dies, resentment takes its place, making the former object of worship hideous to our sight. And when our idols fall, some mysterious inner urge moves us to help them fall yet farther. Certainly, their choices had set the scene, but it was I who finally judged and sentenced them both.

In the shock of that realization, I dropped my empty frame by the lake and ran.

11

In the Hall of the Mountain King

WHY DID I RUN? I would spend the next six weeks trying to answer that question for myself and for the various police investigators and psychiatrists who tried to make sense of my actions and my testimony. It was the housekeeper who had summoned the police, having arrived a little later that morning and discovered Freja in the lake. When the police arrived, and the cottage was searched, Erik's remains were discovered on his bed, reeking of vodka and vomit. An autopsy would reveal heart failure brought about by alcohol poisoning as the cause of death.

Freja's autopsy, however, was not so straightforward. While her cause of death was, naturally, drowning, other details floated to the surface as the investigation continued. Foremost among them was that Freja wasn't Freja at all; she was Lois, and she was 47 years old. Her first marriage was at 18, her second at 28, her third, to Erik, at 38. No one could have guessed that she had been in her twenties for half of her life. Even Erik, although he had inklings of the cost of her immortal beauty, never knew her exact age. She had always remarried at ten-year intervals. Perhaps that is how long it takes for the worship of another human being to fail. According to the pattern, she was coming up due in the next year for another. I will never know what her plans were. Still, I have reason to believe that she was ready to stay, to stop pretending, perhaps even ready to let herself be caught aging a little if Erik had only been content to stop asking about the children she could no longer conceive.

At one of the legal proceedings, I saw an old woman, very frail, but I imagined quite beautiful at one point in her life. Freja had, for the past twenty-nine years, been supporting her mother with the allowances she received from her husbands, all of them well-endowed financially. Now this fragile old woman, left by her husband years ago with a baby she could scarcely support, stood to inherit the majority of Erik and Freja's estate. It did feel like there was a certain kind of victory in Freja's poor mother, spent and abandoned, being so well cared for by her daughter's wealth. But whatever victory one could imagine was eclipsed by the tragedy, not only of a mother surviving her only child but what Freja had to do for the security she had obtained for both of them. Freja's victory, if you could call it that, was indeed a hollow one, as it seems most victories in this life tend to be.

I wonder if Freja's mother ever guessed how much her own life had influenced her daughter's. How Freja's calculated self-protection, which had seemed like the wisdom of learning from her mother's experience, proved to be a death sentence. There was one thing I was sure of: Freja had known at least one real and pure love in her life. Whether or not she had ever loved Erik or her previous husbands, I would never know, but it was clear that she had truly loved her mother.

In later months . . . years . . . my heart would continue to break for Freja as more pieces of her past surfaced to form a more accurate, and tragic picture than I had ever painted of her, this beautiful woman, who tried so hard to escape the passage of time through some of the cruelest methods man has devised. But then, why wouldn't she choose this pain? When the society that created her continues to place beauty and youth as the foremost among female virtues? And I, caught up in the illusion, was convinced that a determined woman practicing yoga every morning by the lake, was a goddess commanding the worship of all nature.

No, the question isn't why she would, but why wouldn't become what she was, since the world so clearly required it of her. And why wouldn't Erik lose his mind, when the same society decrees that men are destined for greatness and eternal fame, virility of mind and body if only they will reach out and lay claim to their own great destinies? The manic delusion of impending greatness—the crushing weight of the belief that he must change the world and leave something of his greatness to posterity.

Erik and Freja were trying to be exactly what they were supposed to be and were perhaps more successful than most. They had found each other, after all. Erik worshipped his own patrilineage and potential. He looked for a partner who could be the true equal of his assumed greatness: An undying spirit—a goddess of eternal youth and beauty who could share in that ideal vision. He found a willing accomplice in Freja, who had been playing that part for some time before his casting her as his own leading lady, but when his vanity and desire for greatness led him to consider the production of an heir, they met an incompatibility. His goddess would have to become less than perfect to bring about his wish. Perhaps they could have survived it, but her advancing age and his physical waste denied the opportunity of finding out. But they knew—of course, they knew—that they were merely being absorbed into this cult of inflated expectations. They realized the truth long before I did, though we all realized the truth too late. Even as I ran in horror that fateful morning into the fringe of trees by the lakeshore, the full weight of that truth was only beginning to bear down on me.

By the time the authorities arrived at the scene, I was some three miles into the mossy corridors of the forest, running like a madman or a fugitive with the devil on my heels. Why did I run? Even as I was running, I couldn't have answered why. I had some mad sense that I must escape, that I was somehow culpable and that the dense canopy of the old-growth forest was my only hope for escaping judgment. I ran with what seemed to me like superhuman speed and endurance. I ran as I'd never run before and never have since. At one point, my toe caught a root, and I fell hard, gouging the heels of my hands and biting my tongue as my chin struck the ground. I scrambled back up and ran on, my hands throbbing, and the taste of blood in my mouth.

I ran all day until the darkness came, and even in the dark, I slowly groped through the undergrowth until I reached a stream. It was only with my face plunged into the cold water gulping greedily that I realized how thirsty I had been, my throat aching with dry and weeping. When I'd finally had my fill, I collapsed, curled against the protruding root of a towering, ancient Douglas fir in a shallow, mossy nest. The darkness was teeming with irrational fears, and it was then that I realized, finally, that the abyss I had been philosophizing about, perceiving in the periphery of my mind, was not something external to me. It was hell. I was in it as much as it was in me.

I slept almost instantly, but my mind ran on into the night. In my dreams, I was pursued deeper and deeper into the woods by an angry Mountain King. I could hear his heavy footfalls pursuing me, and I could see his vast hands sweeping aside the ancient trees like stalks of wheat, calling my name and accusing me:

"You human-things—you're all the same . . .

. . . you really think your thoughts don't matter?"

In my dream, I knew it was true. By thinking it, wishing it, wanting it, sure enough, I had done it! I had murdered them with my mind and its morbid machinations. Let me out! I wish I could wake up! This can't be me! I can't accept that this is me! Free me from this moment. Let me live in the past, the future, even a convincing falsehood, but spare me the emptiness of this present moment that exposes me for what I really am! Save me! Rescue me! Repair me! Restore me! Or else annihilate me altogether, for I cannot bear the awareness of this thing that is me! I tried to scream inwardly in my dreams, but no sound would come. I screamed in silence throughout that night under the fir tree.

Early in the morning, as the sun was coming up, I was awakened by a cold, wet snuffling nose thrust in my ear. That rude sensation was followed closely by the thundering bay of a scent hound that had discovered its quarry sleeping under a tree. Its bay sent the roosting birds flying from the treetops in a panic. The rest was confinement. And questions.

It was prison first until the preponderance of evidence convinced the authorities that my confession was invalid. But I had! I had so obviously, so maliciously, murdered them! Erik had, himself, carried out the last motions of the deed, but I had orchestrated the action, plotted it, without even realizing it or admitting it to myself until my lack of surprise brought home to me the force of my own influence. Why wouldn't they believe me and give me my just punishment? After all, I had earned it and no longer wished to escape it.

After prison, I was transferred to a psychiatric hospital in Seattle. Interviews. Observations. Thanks mainly to a widespread paradigm shift emphasizing a pattern of diathesis and stress as a way to explain the multiple causes of schizophrenia, the team of psychiatrists assigned to my case came to a swift conclusion regarding my diagnosis. Although I had no family history or record indicating mental illness, it was concluded that I had a diathesis—a predisposition—let us say a seed of paranoid schizophrenia buried somewhere deep in my psyche. It had hitherto lain dormant until it was activated by a certain perfect storm of stressors. In short, the tragic murder-suicide of my friends while I was staying with them. This event, they concluded, translated my diathesis into an actual disorder. I was ill, they said. Very ill, indeed.

But no! I was not ill! I was emotionally distraught. I was a mess, in fact. I had tried, and I still wanted to confess to the authorities how my own thoughts had created this tragic situation. I was truly to blame, and I would not accept the evidence provided by the coroner's office and the police, that I was not culpable for their deaths. My refusal of this evidence was interpreted by my care providers, however, as a delusion of guilt—the development of an idea of reference. I had assigned the tragic happenings of my friends' lives to my own delusional framework, assigning my thoughts a sense of power and significance that they did not, in reality, possess.

They gave me pills.

"Why do you blame yourself? You're clearly innocent. Look at your own diary—your own words. What virtuous thoughts and wishes to help your struggling friend. You're a good person who wanted to do a nice thing for your friend. It just didn't work, but that's not your fault." They said it was shock. Shock and stress had muddled my brain into thinking I was guilty when I was truly innocent. Grief had darkened my inner eye and caused me to lose my grip on the facts of what had happened, inventing a false version.

"But don't you know? The facts mean nothing! It's the truth that matters! You don't know what my inner eye has seen! My past and my future condemn me! I condemn myself!" They continued to try to convince me of my innocence, ever referencing my own journal entries as though they were somehow irrefutable evidence of how pure my motives had been. Their approval of what they thought my motives were only stung worse in my already wounded conscience—a conscience that now knew its own guilt beyond all doubt.

"You have a creative mind—beautifully imaginative. You know it is a special gift, but you have to use it carefully. You've imagined a false scenario. You've imagined your thoughts to be far more influential than they are. Thoughts are just thoughts. They're insubstantial. Yours just happen to be very colorful, because you're an artist and you're stressed."

"You don't know! You don't know how poisonous my thoughts have been! Poisonous!" I continued to try to convince them of my guilt until the pills made me withdraw into myself and refuse to speak anymore.

Indeed, the pills caused me to sleep, and even when I was awake, my mind still slept as my body went about its duties. The rapid, guilty thoughts had been distressing, but they melted away until my mind was like a quiet cave in absolute darkness. No thoughts could penetrate that obscurity, and I spent my days staring straight ahead or sleeping.

They experimented with different doses and drugs and eventually with electric shocks until, in the end, I learned to pretend. I learned to answer their questions in a way that was pleasing to them: "I'm not guilty of my friends' deaths. I am simply very sad, having witnessed a terrible crime involving people I cared about, but I will continue to feel better as time goes by. I will stop blaming myself for this unfortunate event, which was in no way my fault or my doing. I will go home. I will live my life. I will make new friends and get daily exercise and sunshine. Most of all, I will stop confessing to a crime I didn't commit. I am sad, but I am innocent."

I said the words convincingly enough, but in my mind, I argued: Their bodies feed the forest, along with my innocence, which perished with them. I know now what I am and what I ought to have been. I know how my life is intertwined with their death, and no amount of psychoanalysis can dissociate my thoughts from the end they set in motion. Regardless of how the laws of men interpret blame, I am culpable, but they will not grant me the punishment I deserve. They will not allow me the grief I have brought upon myself through worship misapplied, which mutated, as it had to, into hatred. Only I know. Only I shout in silence that I've done this thing . . . that this is what my thinking did. You, all of you analyzing the workings of my cerebral cortex, you simply haven't learned yet that our thoughts are everything. It is our thoughts that, like some infection, start small, but when we indulge them, they grow to such an all-consuming power that they endanger our very being and those around us. Erik and Freja are dead because I wished it, and through wishing it, I subtly, subconsciously, set the scene for them to carry out the climactic action themselves. My mind begot a murder.

Babushka, her words on that last day together in the woods kept haunting me:

> "Many mushrooms try to disguise themselves like the tasty, wholesome ones, but they are really poisonous and could be the last thing you ever eat. For every tasty mushroom, there are a hundred others that will kill you. So take care. Take every mushroom in your hand—examine it closely—but do not put every mushroom in your basket."

That boy was me, still seeing only the surface of things, and thinking that day, that lesson, so long ago, had been about identifying edible wild mushrooms. "Mind your thoughts, Eliasz. Mind—your—thoughts." The hermit's wild, blue eyes saw through me. But who can say such things aloud in this place without condemning himself to more experiments? Who can say these things that are wisdom without seeming insane? Who can talk about the reality of dragons and monsters and poisonous mushrooms without sealing his own medicated fate? I finally said what they wanted to hear, and they sent me home.

12

2020: The Radiant Darkness

GRIEF IS A STRANGE animal. It's most cruel and most vicious in the first year. Then, as it fades to the outer edges of your consciousness and you think you've moved on, you catch it in the corner of your eye, smell it on occasional breezes, and hear it in the notes of particular songs. It's never really gone; it only ever becomes less acute, less immediate.

Life goes on as if nothing ever happened. Seasons come and go; flowers bloom and fade; snow falls and melts; and the sun shines on us all—guilty and innocent—living and dead. The world is quite insane, how it just keeps spinning in space in spite of everything. If it had any sense of justice, it would come to a full stop and let the Void consume us all. But on it goes, and we're left to clear up the wreckage of our misadventures as best we can and keep getting up every morning. That's what I did, I suppose. Condemned to life. Forty-four years. Has it really been that long?

I'm sitting on a ferry, the old man with the leather-bound journal and pen, artifacts in themselves of an era long dead. It feels as though only the strait of Juan de Fuca is older than me. I look around at a familiar scene, but altered as well, as time alters everything. I look out at a mass of young heads, bowed in reverence over glowing screens, filling the Void with webs of connections and faces, all speaking at once, some screaming into the darkness for someone to notice. Intimate thoughts, narcissism, nonsense, profanity, and the wisdom of the dead, ripped from its context and expanding through space—fading to nothing but mere worthless remains of something once beautiful. Generations blossom, ripen, and wither, like the passing seasons giving life to the next, the new, who ask the same terrifying question, look into the same darkness and fling their sacrifices into its vacuous jaws. There are always new ways to fill a hole. And the ferry plunges on forward through the waves as it must.

I never thought I would have the courage to come back here. I see now the necessity if only to swing an imaginary sword at imaginary ghosts, putting them, finally, to rest.

I am here now. I have arrived.

There is always something to be felt in every place one goes. Sometimes we are more sensitive to it than other times. I remember entering a small church as a young boy, a Russian Orthodox mission down a narrow street in the heart of New York City. My mother took me one dark evening in wintertime after the commotion of Christmas had died down, and the remains of winter stretched before us like a road with no turning. Great Vespers on the eve of Theophany: one of my warmest memories of our first year in New York.

There were only seven people—the priest, a sub-deacon, an older man and woman constituting a choir, my mother and I, and a young man whose thick beard and style of clothes suggested he was newly arrived from the Motherland. The room smelled of melting beeswax. My mother lifted me up to kiss the icon of the Mother of God Vladimir, who looked back at me tenderly as she held the tiny Christ in her arms, their cheeks pressed together. Mama lit a candle and made the sign of the cross several times, touching the cold stone floor with her red, calloused hand. I sat on the floor in a corner, holding a little notebook and pencil, drawing sunny scenes of a cottage near a deep primeval wood in Eastern Poland, while the service echoed through the little room.

Although there were so few voices, it sounded like the church was full. Who knows how children sense these things, but for the first time, a conscious thought entered my supple little mind: that this tiny chapel was somehow altered by the prayers that floated upward like the curling, sweet-smelling smoke from the censer as it jingled like sleigh-bells in the night. The prayers lingered in that sweet smell, and like a sponge, the building itself and the people in it absorbed them and were transfigured by them. The little trees newly planted the previous spring in the small garden in the back of the church seemed to take strength from the constant prayers that flowed from that little Russian church, and the glow of the beeswax candles seemed to warm the entire cold city that night

That memory returns to me in all clarity, the smell of beeswax and incense, as I sit here on Freja's rock, looking out at the black lake. The cottage is still standing on the pebbly shore. New tenants have taken it, made updates, made it their own. Do they feel it when they sit still on their deck chairs? Do they sense it when they look at the trees and rocks and water? Or is it just because I know—because I was there and played a part? My heart sinks, and my mind is disturbed as I look at this familiar scene. The trees, so often sources of great joy in life, feel all wrong and defiled, as though they have witnessed a terrible act of violence. They are still, like death, standing in a place of sickening soil. They, the new tenants, don't know what monstrous things happened in this place, but the innocent rocks and trees, they do remember it and have absorbed its foul stench. They seem to scream, these silent witnesses, for us to Become, Become, Become. Become what we must be—to save them from our transgressions. We hurt them. We hurt ourselves. We hurt the entire landscape and all of humanity with the bitter fruit of our wild thoughts. I wish I could comfort them. How does one comfort a tree with hands still dripping with blood? Forgive me. Forgive me.

May God forgive us all.

A flock of clouds has just obscured the sun, and I see the shadow flying across the face of the water. Just a shadow. How perspective changes things! I think I see it now. Oh, my dear Passerby! I have spent my years staring into a void that was only ever a shadow. What I perceived to be a great concavity, has always been a great convexity—a trick of perspective—equivocal space made clear with time and distance. You can't fill something that is already full. Two objects cannot occupy the same space at the same time . . . or can they? What am I trying to say? We were all wrong, feverishly filling, covering, ignoring a hole that was never a hole.

Should I tell the secret of the Void as I've seen it? It's not a void at all but at once a shadow and a blinding light, a radiant darkness, both heaven, and hell, depending on one's state of soul. It is the evidence, or perhaps just the absolute intangible conviction of the existence of something beyond all existence, too vast to be seen or described in words, too simple to be understood. Does that frighten you? Does it frighten you more than if there were nothing there at all? Or does it give you comfort? For my part, I can't decide. I can only speak as a madman in a maze who has run terror-stricken through this seemingly chaotic meaninglessness sustained only by the faint and secret hope that at the end of each turn, I might finally experience Theophany. That I might truly understand the wise words of my grandparents, the faces of the saints in the corner, and the answer to the problem of worship. All that is left for this tired old man is to round the last bend and draw near the edge. To finally peer with hope into that blindingly radiant darkness and into the mystery where all discursive knowledge withers and falls silent.